Lost

Among

the Tide

TAMMY B. TSONIS

This is a work of fiction. Names, characters, events, and incidents are either products of the author's imagination or are used fictitiously. Any resemblance to actual persons, living or dead, or actual events is purely coincidental.

Cover by Wynter Designs

ISBN: 978-0-578-83556-3

DEDICATION

For my family and friends who believed in me when I didn't.
And to all the missed opportunities that inspire us along the way.

CHAPTER ONE

An Artie Shaw tune resonated from the gramophone's brass-colored horn. As the record spun round, the static that bridged the gap between then and now accompanied the once-smooth crooner's voice. It was nostalgic to anyone sixty years my senior, but the brash blow of the horn was nothing new. The arrangement wasn't among the usual tunes I had heard from my grandmother's collection, but it still brought me back to my childhood and the many times I'd sat there, music transporting me to a different time. The lightheartedness of the harmony transcended space and time, like many of those songs often had, if only to offer an escape from the realities of war. A strange sense of comfort washed over me every time she played those songs from her neatly kept living room, untouched by time.

My grandmother slowly lifted the brass tip with her shaky finger and replaced the record with Shaw's rendition of *At Sundown.* Her face lit up like a bright cloudless sky after a turbulent summer storm. The years seemed to fade from her face with every lively beat, and in its place was a glimpse of youth in her faded olive eyes.

She bore the burden of old age, no doubt, holding on tight to the chair's wooden armrests. The fabric's golden background and once-bright-rose floral pattern now faded to a pale shade of dusk. The historic chestnut panels surrounding the fireplace were an enchanting backdrop to the room frozen in time. She looked up and smiled at me the same way she always had, with kind and inviting eyes that made me feel as if they could wrap me up in their happiness. At times, I yearned to see them in their prime, when they were brighter with a hint of sparkle, like the lapping waves of the ocean in the early morning sun, reflecting a thirst of youthful adventure. They had many stories to tell; I knew from experience.

On those days she tucked me into bed as a child, each story became a bigger piece of a puzzle that I couldn't wait to unravel.

"What's wrong, my dear Rebecca" she asked.

"Nothing, just a heavy heart, I guess."

I wasn't sure how interested my grandmother would be in the fickle thoughts of a single woman.

"It has to be something quite important for you to be so distant. You've always been able to tell me what was on your mind ever since you were a little girl."

That was true. My grandmother had a knack for bringing out my deepest secrets, even at an early age. I remember sitting on a tall wooden stool in her kitchen, baking cakes while listening to an early Frank Sinatra tune. She would sing a few verses while delicately folding the ingredients into her batter, each stroke a velvet ribbon enveloping her spatula. The anticipation of sweets would elicit a confession every time, however innocent, from my lips. Whether it was blaming my sister, Colleen, when I broke my mother's colored-glass jewelry box or gushing my heart out about my latest school crush, the words never failed to pour out of my mouth, just like the cake batter filling her empty pans.

"I just have a lot on my mind. It's nothing I haven't caused myself." I said, trying to look away from my grandmother's gaze.

"The two of us are very similar, you know I felt that way many times when I was young—always the complicated one. My brother was easy going, comfortable with what he had and where he lived. I wanted more for myself, but those days it was frowned upon. I suppose I was always looking for adventure but was a little too scared to follow through." She let out a hardy chuckle that deepened the lines around her lips and eyes.

"You know how much I love your stories, Grandma." I couldn't help but smile in anticipation.

That chuckle always signaled the start of an interesting story. It had been that way ever since I could remember.

Grandma Helen slowly rose from her chair and headed straight to the gramophone once more. She placed another thirty-three with a classic from Jimmy Dorsey, *Stompin' at the Savoy.*

She slowly sat down on her faded chair, folding her frail fingers into one another. A big smile lit up her face, instantly reversing the years from her aged demeanor.

"Newport?" I asked, knowing this particular story would be about a place that held special memories for her—Newport, Rhode Island.

"Yes," she replied. "The City by the Sea. It's a beautiful place that lingers in your soul long after you've left. The sapphire-colored ocean takes your breath away every time. If you're lucky enough to live close to its beaches, the sound of the swaying waves will lull you softly to sleep and awaken you in the morning with its distant whisper.

"I first visited Newport during the war when it had lost its Gilded-Age splendor. What was once a summer retreat for the wealthy soon became an area heavily affected by economic turmoil. Although the beautiful mansions were closed and forgotten, it still continued to be a breathtaking place, rich with history and natural beauty like no other.

"I found myself there, one year, when my family took a detour from our usual summer vacation with Aunt Edna in Boston. I fell in love with the beaches and the cobblestone streets lined with historic buildings that dated back to the Seventeen Hundreds. In fact, I fell in love more than once that year." She smiled a girlish smile that lit up her faded eyes.

"This is about a man, isn't it?" I asked, clearly aware of the answer.

That shy twinkle was not unique, but rather a common secret gesture shared by every woman who had ever fallen in love once or twice in her lifetime.

"Yes, but it's so much more," she whispered. This time the girlish smile revealed a sense of nostalgia. "The human heart is as vast and complex as the ocean, my dear. Our experiences and relationships aren't always black and white, and oftentimes we only realize it when we look back. It's a wonderful thing to be able to remember your precious moments long after they've passed. All those emotions flood back with each memory. Those precious moments are locked away deep in your subconscious like a forgotten shipwreck at the bottom of the ocean floor away from the light of day for years and years. Then, one day, they float to the top and reveal themselves just as clear as when you experienced them the first time."

Grandma went on to describe the natural beauty of this special place—the ten-mile winding road of Ocean Drive, and the clear-blue water crashing into the dark-espresso rocks of that charming historic town in picturesque New England. The grand mansions on Bellevue, radiating with beauty, were never truly forgotten. Decades later, they were brought back to life and treasured, as if they had never been lost.

"Have you ever seen the ocean at night, Rebecca? The darkness seems to swallow it entirely at first glance, but after a closer look the ocean simply fools the observer. Its waves continue to crash just as strong. Its white tops continue to soak the nearby rocks. On an ethereal moonlit night, the waves illuminate the water like a flashlight streaming through a dense forest."

"It sounds beautiful." I couldn't hide my anticipation for the rest of her story. "And?"

"Yes, I will tell you how I met the man I would remember for the rest of my life.

"People come and go in your life throughout the years, but few truly stay in your heart and mind permanently. Those are the people you were meant to meet, and their impact will stay with you long after they're gone from your life. The simplest thing will remind you of them. Some think it's a curse to remember someone who's no longer there, but I think it's a gift. You will replay those happy moments over and over again, sometimes remembering the tiniest detail. It allows you the pleasure of reliving them again, ever so briefly." She smiled her famous gentle smile, seemingly content to have those special memories with her even at the ripe old age of ninety-three.

Part I

CHAPTER TWO

Newport 1943

I met James while strolling the local shops on Thames Street with my cousin Elizabeth, one afternoon. Lizzie and I were inseparable that summer. I hadn't seen her in years, but it seemed that that absence just melted away, like a popsicle on a hot summer day, as soon as we saw one another again. She was the only girl in a family of three boys, and sometimes I think she missed not having another girl around. When we were little girls, we used to play for hours together after school. Her family lived a few streets down from our house in Waterbury, Connecticut, but they had to move when I was twelve. I was so heartbroken to see Lizzie go.

After all, we were as close as sisters.

Seven years later, we finally reunited in Newport. We headed to First Beach together as soon as I arrived. I was eager to enjoy the sun and the sound of the waves. By then, Elizabeth had become a beach bum of sorts and found every opportunity to introduce me to the easy-going lifestyle she'd grown to love. We spent the first three days in the same daily routine—beach in the morning, shops on Bellevue and Lower Thames Street in the afternoon, the beach after dinner at Aunt Edna's, and a movie at the Paramount Theater on Broadway at night.

James caught my eye, one afternoon, during one of our walks. He was walking along Bellevue with two other naval officers, all dressed in their khaki uniforms. We spied them from across the street as they nodded and smiled at the female passersby who were trying to get their attention. With the Naval War College on the mainland and the Torpedo Station on nearby Goat Island, men in uniform were a common sight. Like many of the other sailors in town during the war, they were out on liberty, trying to forget what lay ahead of them. It was an uncertain time, and making the most of their free time was what most sailors did.

Elizabeth and I were young—I was nineteen and she was twenty. Of course, being young and foolish, we got a little giddy every time we saw those handsome fellas in their uniforms. Groups of them would walk around in the afternoon and early evenings. Elizabeth would nudge me with her elbow, pointing out the one she thought was the smartest, handsomest, and strongest.

"Look at that blond-haired sailor over there." She would signal with a nod of her head. "I bet he has a girl at every port. That smirk and brash attitude says it all. He's certainly handsome enough. And the red-haired one with the bulky build? He's trying to be as smooth as his friend, but that nervous laugh says he spends most of his free time with books instead of girls."

Hearing those descriptions was often the highlight of my day. We chuckled a little too loud at times, and the subjects of our conversations would turn to us with disapproving scowls on their faces. I was always the first one to get embarrassed, but nothing deterred Elizabeth from ogling even more.

We secretly followed James and his friends to La Forge Restaurant in the old casino on Bellevue that same afternoon. We were feeling a bit hungry, so we decided to take a lunch break ourselves.

I've heard the restaurant still stands today. Its décor is reminiscent of my days—the mahogany trim, mirrored glass, and pastel-green booths all take you back to a time when hats were a must and people dressed up in public.

The fellas were laughing and toasting only two tables down the aisle from us. We whispered to each other, commenting on who we thought was the most handsome and giggled a little too loud, as usual.

James was the first to turn around and look our way. I'm sure Elizabeth and I blushed as red as ripe tomatoes under the afternoon sun. I could feel my cheeks burning, but I couldn't resist looking up. I saw him look right at me with the handsomest smile I'd ever seen—his bright blue eyes the same shade of sapphire as the waves of the ocean, and just as captivating. I was instantly smitten.

He walked over, leaving his friends behind, and asked if we were from the area. I replied *no* before Elizabeth could admit she was a local. He offered to give me the local's tour of the town, and of course, I didn't hesitate to say *yes*. It wasn't long before James picked me up from Aunt Edna's between training every day and showed me the sights of the town that he'd spent most of his youth tromping around in. He wasn't afraid to have an adventure or two and he confessed all the thrilling details as he pointed each place out to me.

James had grown up in Newport—the son of a naval officer trained by the US Naval War College. As the oldest, James was expected to join the Navy like his father had. And he'd accepted the role of pursuing a military career but never quite felt fulfilled by it. His father was often quick-tempered and rarely showed affection towards either one of his sons. Any sign of affection or emotion was seen as cowardly and had no place in his household. He was raising young sailors who would one day become great naval officers. James and his brother, Frank, were ordered to read up on military history and geography so they could prepare for a rewarding military career. Their father had big plans for his sons, whether they liked it or not.

He'd often test them on battle facts as soon as he came through the door after work to check that they weren't disobeying his authority. I suppose his intentions were good, but the boys experienced their father's wrath when it was obvious they hadn't studied. James was often left to do extra chores or undergo an occasional beating as punishment for disobeying his father's orders. Their father lived and breathed the military and expected his sons to do the same.

"A squadron never goes to war unprepared, and so too should a man prepare himself for what's ahead. You'll thank me when you're older," James would recite, mimicking his father's voice.

James hated reading the textbooks his father would bring them. He longed to be outside, free to explore the rugged scenery on his own terms. When their father was away on military missions, the two brothers spent most of their time outdoors from sunrise to sundown, only to come home for a quick lunch before heading back to the beach or to hike a trail or two. Their mother reminded them to keep up their reading while their father was gone to avoid his punishments, but she couldn't resist giving them her blessing.

James ultimately went into the service, and Frank later left Newport for Providence where he took a job as a bookkeeper. Frank hated the pressures from their father. He was determined to start his own life away from Aquidneck Island and, one day, decided to pursue his dreams. Although they lived miles apart, the two brothers remained close and met up often when James wasn't training.

"It's what I'm expected to do. It's not all bad and the best part is that I can see the world," he told me once. "If I had my way, I would spend my days traveling and capturing the beauty of the world with my camera. There's so much culture and natural beauty around us, not even a war could change that." His eyes reflected a darker shade of blue, as his mood grew somber.

Ocean Drive was the first place James took me. The ten-mile winding road was a magnificent sight that stretched from Bellevue Avenue to Castle Hill's historic lighthouse. The breathtaking drive houses some of the oldest mansions and manors in Newport. The jewel of it all, of course, was the most majestic view of the Atlantic Ocean I had ever seen. That sapphire water glistened under the warm afternoon sun, while the cool, salty breeze awakened my senses like a rainstorm after a long summer drought. The sound of the crashing waves against the rocky coastline made me feel alive and free. It was exhilarating being at the edge of the earth surrounded by such a powerful and serene wonder.

I laughed with excitement at how close those crashing waves were. It was nothing I'd experienced before living in my small Connecticut town. There was nothing to protect you from the wind and its strength. It was wild and bare, and it sent tingles up my spine.

I couldn't remember another time I had felt so free and happy —James driving by my side with the top down on his ivory nineteen-forties Plymouth Coupe, his short chestnut hair gently swaying in the wind. He smiled back at me briefly, holding the steering wheel tight as he made each narrow, winding turn. He knew I enjoyed it as much as he always had.

We parked along the side of the road, like many couples there enjoying the mild summer day had. James opened the driver's side door, jumped out, and opened mine. With a mischievous smile, he took my hand and led me to the water.

"Let's get up close," he whispered in my ear.

As he held my hand, I couldn't help but feel like the luckiest girl on the island. The wind swept through the rolls neatly set in place on my head, replacing them with wild waves mimicking the strong ocean surf.

We strolled along the Drive—what the locals called it—and chatted about our families, and how things would be after the war. I told him how bored I was working as a store clerk for our local clothes shop. I wanted to go back to school to become a history teacher.

"There is nothing better than education," my father would say. Even though he had grown up a farmer and ran a modest grocery shop as an adult, he knew education provided a world of opportunities, even for a woman. He was quite ahead of his time.

"He sounds like a great man. Someone I'd like to meet one day." James winked and gave me a sly smile, making my heart skip a beat. I looked away as my cheeks flushed.

We continued our walk, climbing the enormous rocks that were swept by the surf in a rhythmic pattern. Their surfaces glistened in the sun, intensifying the contrast of the ebony and ash-colored rocks against the bright blue ocean. The seagulls soared high in the cloudless sky.

How envious I was of those seagulls, spending their days among the ocean's magnificent presence! They soared towards the horizon where the line between sky and ocean disappeared in a blur. Their cries faded slowly, absorbed by the sound of the crashing waves.

"Isn't the water beautiful today, Helen?" he asked. His

bright eyes reflected the excitement of the water.

"It is." I couldn't take my eyes off the rush of the surf.

"I come out here by myself as often as I can. It helps me think. I don't know what I'm doing sometimes, but somehow this spot makes everything better even if it's only for a moment." James turned to me, observing my temporary withdrawal from the world, and slowly reached out for my hand. "You seem a million miles away."

"Just lost in the beauty around me," I responded, still mesmerized by the scenery.

I looked down, and saw his hand lying comfortably on mine, as if it had found a forever-home there.

"Just as I am," he said, pulling me closer and caressing my flushed cheeks with his other hand. As if in a dream, his lips touch mine, slowly at first, then more passionately—like a rush of water filling an empty basin. His breath was warm and intense, heating my soul along with my heart.

It became the start of an exciting time in my life, filled with happy moments. Until it ended, that is.

CHAPTER THREE

Summer in Newport

The next month, James and I became inseparable. We spent most of our afternoons together, getting to know each other between his drills and trainings. As promised, he showed me where the locals relaxed, what they ate, and the hidden gems like Second Beach or "Reject Beach," as many referred to it; Hanging Rock, and the Purgatory Chasm—a hidden cleft formation on the cliffs of Second Beach.

Second Beach—James' favorite—was just as stunning as any of the other beaches in town, its waves just as strong, and sand just as fine. It was located in Middletown, a bit outside Newport, but not as popular as the exclusive Bailey's Beach or the famous

Easton's Beach that was just up the road. Its crescent shape mimicked that of Easton's, but on a smaller and more intimate scale.

James and Frank would spend their entire summer at Second Beach, swimming in the water for hours on end and playing football in the sand. They hiked the chasm and Hanging Rock until sundown, betting on who would make it to the top first. During one of their visits when they were teenagers, both of them got hurt while hiking up the rock. James scraped his upper-right cheek, and Frank his left. They both avoided their father for a week, worried that he'd catch on to their escapades. He never did find out, however, and proudly assumed it was a precursor to his sons' winning hooks to an aggressor's jaw. It was rare to hear a hint of pride in their father's voice, so the brothers couldn't help but savor the moment and keep the truth to themselves as long as possible.

"I had such great times here with Frank and my friends when I was younger," he confessed during one of our trips there. "I'm going to miss Newport when I'm gone. I hope it misses me."

"It will," I reassured him. "And I will too, every day until you come back to me."

I kissed his lips, holding him close as I tried to hold on to the moment as long as I could.

I knew from the beginning our time together was short. One day, we'd no longer walk that stretch of sand together, our fingers would no longer interlock as one. Instead, I would walk alone, aware of the deafening emptiness around me. I tried as hard as I could not to think about that, but the thought always remained in the back of my mind. There were times I would stare off at the water contemplating it. James' only reply was a sad smile and an outstretched arm to pull me close.

"The ocean is the one constant in our lives. It's shade of blue changes as quickly as the placid sky, but nothing can take away its vastness and serenity. Its waves will hypnotically sway back and forth in the same drawn-out rhythm today and every day, even a hundred years from now. That's one thing that the war can never change." His eyes grew darker as his thoughts took him far from the moment.

"There are still lots of other good things in the world," I stated, trying to comfort him and distract him from those worrisome thoughts.

It was a habit I'd inherited from my father. We both had a tendency to reflect on the positive side of things as a way to provide comfort to the people around us, and maybe ourselves even more so. I tried not to make it too obvious, but I hoped James would think of me as an important reason to come back home.

It seemed to work. He shook off his negative thoughts as quickly as they'd come, and as fast as the changing wind. He stood up, gave me one of his sly smiles, and grabbed my hand, then led me to the edge of the surf where we splashed into an oncoming wave. We got drenched in the cool early-summer water.

He quickly handed me a blanket that he'd pulled out of his car, wrapped it around me, and brought me closer, embracing me with strong arms and holding me to his chest until I stopped shivering. I could hear his heart racing, loud and strong, like the humming of a brand-new engine in its prime. I was safe, warm, and happy, and I never wanted to leave.

CHAPTER FOUR

One Last Hurrah

Before he left for war, we attended a grand party held by the senior officers at the officers' club. Everyone was dressed to impress—the men in their formal uniforms and the ladies in long, sequined dresses. The officers' club had a large banquet room decorated for the grandest of receptions. Crystal chandlers adorned the ceiling, while the newly waxed floors reflected the scattered light throughout the room. It was a party to end all parties, it seemed.

Ladies twirled on the dance floor, their skirts spinning round like colorful pinwheels in the wind. Their handsome partners pulled them closer with every spin, smiling more seductively as their eyes met. Laughter and happiness filled the entire room while the navy band brought alive the swinging music of the time. The sound echoed throughout the room, erasing any thought of the troubled times ahead.

James was light on his feet. His steps echoed every beat of the music perfectly. I had a difficult time keeping up, and a few of my missteps landed on his toes. My cheeks flushed, but he laughed it off and told me it was part of my charm. We danced most of the night, enjoying the music and each other's company. The only breaks we took were to share appetizers and drinks with the other military couples.

James had a way with people, and it was incredibly apparent at the party. He easily transitioned from one conversation to another, genuinely recalling something memorable about the person he was speaking to every time. He made everyone feel like the only person in the room, and I felt even more privileged to be at his side.

After dinner and a few trips to the dance floor, I snuck away to the ladies' room to freshen up. The victory curls that had been set in place atop my head were now a floppy mess, and my crimson lipstick had begun to fade. I looked at my reflection in the mirror and couldn't help but think what a blissful dream I was living. It was a wonderful, but incredibly bittersweet feeling. The man I had grown to love would leave the next day.

As I walked back to the dance floor, James stood near the dessert table, glancing over at me with a smile and a wink, his hands tucked away in his pockets, feet stretched out and crossed in front of him. Relaxed and content. It was one of the first times I had seen him completely at ease away from the ocean.

He often had the excitement of a little boy exploring a new toy, and it was contagious to everyone around him. I couldn't help but feel that excitement as he described the happy memories he had in Newport. He was a free spirit like no other I had met before. To be able to live in the moment was a gift not many people could fully understand, but he did, somehow.

I envied everything about him. I was the complete opposite—always worrying about what would happen five steps ahead. Being with James somehow eased that burden. It allowed me to forget the ugliness in the world and focus on the fleeting moments of my splendid present.

As I approached him, he gently wrapped his arm around the curve of my waist and brought me close. After a brief welcome back kiss, we walked back to the dance floor as the music became more melodic. The songs became slower and the singer's voice gentler; he sang, *Till Then* by the Mills Brothers. The lyrics replayed in my dreams for months.

James held my hand in his, his cheek gently touching mine as he brought me closer. I could smell his cologne as he drew near. The familiar scent of warm, rich amber wood, and a faint sea scent filled my senses. I wanted it to last a lifetime.

"Will you wait for me?" he whispered in my ear, repeating the lyrics of the song.

"Of course."

The words spilled from my lips without a thought. I remember feeling joy one minute and dread the next. I touched his check gently and studied his every feature—the shade of blue in his almond shaped eyes, the faded scar on his right cheek, the strong dimpled chin, and the curve of his lips as he smiled back at me. I wanted to remember his face every time I closed my eyes.

East Providence 2016

"I waited for him just as promised. He wrote me twelve letters while he was away. Each letter described the splendor he had seen in Europe, from resplendent cathedral churches and palaces in Brussels, to the fragrant countryside of Normandy. He had the opportunity to see the world like he had always wanted to, even though it was only for a short time," my grandmother revealed, as she handed me a letter,

My Dearest Helen,

I have never seen such ornate and intricate architecture as I have here. Only an artist could dream up such beauty and painstakingly carve this much detail in just an ordinary public building.

If I had such talent, you would be my muse. I would make our home look as grand as the fancy cottages of Newport! Each detail would be inspired by the curves of your body and the delicate lines that adorn your lips. How I wish I could trace them with my fingertips once more! How I long to have you close again and feel your warm embrace.

Lovingly Yours,

James

"I waited for each new letter, counting the days and weeks until I would hear back from the man who I thought I would share my life with. Each letter brought us closer, even though we were thousands of miles apart. He was so enthusiastic in the beginning, marveling at the sites he saw and planning our future together. He told me all about the places we would travel to. With each letter, however, that spirit faded, replaced by worry and fear as the war progressed and destroyed many of the opulent cities he saw." She handed me another envelope, yellowed and creased with age.

My Darling Helen,

We are heavily immersed in fighting the "good fight." The casualties are many. We recently lost one of the greatest men I've ever met. He was a great seaman and trumpet player. He did a great impersonation of Bob Hope. That helped us all take our minds off things when we weren't fighting. The only thing better than his jokes was his music. He often played "I Can't Get Started" as we winded down for the night and woke us up for an energized day with his rendition of "When the Saints Go Marching In." Every morning, I see his trumpet lying on his old cot next to a pair of dusty, worn work boots. That's all that's left of him now. What a cruel world we live in, to have such a young, honorable man's life taken away in a matter of seconds!

How I wish I could see and trace your delicate features, to gently touch your windswept hair. It distracts me ever so briefly from these wretched days. I stare at your picture every night, but the short happiness I feel is only followed by a growing sense of heartache and longing. How wonderful it would be to lie next to you at the beach—your sun-kissed skin dressed in sand and salt water on a warm summer's day.

I dread the morning and hurriedly welcome sleep, for it's the only time I get to see you. I dream about our life together—the wonderful memories we'll make and the places we'll travel to someday. I hope I'll be lucky enough to be in your arms again. It's difficult not to wonder if I, too, will succumb to death here. It lurks around us, watching and waiting for the next victim to fall into its terrible clutches. I pray that I'm always able to escape it. If something should happen, know that I love you now, and always will, as long as the ocean meets the horizon.

Lovingly Yours,

James

I couldn't help but smile at the beautiful words that James had written to my grandmother. How lucky she was to have someone who loved her so deeply that it transcended time and distance. She handed me another letter from the very bottom of her pile. Her eyes no longer reflected that youthful spark, but rather a gaze of tiredness and dread. I held my breath.

Dear Helen,

I hope this finds you well. I apologize in advance, and hope you're not offended by receiving a letter from a man you've never met. Knowing my brother, I'm sure he has mentioned me at least once.

It's with a heavy heart that I write you this letter. A few days ago, we were informed that James has gone missing. It hasn't been long, so we're hoping he'll return to us shortly, safe and sound. My brother has spoken fondly of you in our correspondence, and I thought it right to notify you of his disappearance. I am in Newport, trying to console my distraught parents until we hear more news. I will write as soon as we do.

Sincerely,

Frank Simas

"Simas?" I mumbled under my breath.

"Is everything ok, Rebecca?"

"Yes," I lied. It seemed a strange coincidence that there were two Frank Simases in the New England area, let alone in the country. Simas wasn't a common last name, but maybe it wasn't too far-fetched, since there was a sizable Portuguese community on the East Coast.

"I knew I had to see him," Grandma said. "I could only

imagine how difficult it was to have his only brother missing, especially when they had been so close throughout their lives. Frank was nice enough to write me. The least I could do was try to help as best I could. The very next day, I headed to the gray colonial James had pointed out during our walks."

CHAPTER FIVE

Meeting Frank

Time stood still as I walked towards James' childhood home. I could hear my heart beating faster with every step I took. Relief and dread filled my every thought. It was the longest walk I ever had to take.

When I got there, the dark blue door seemed to stare back at me with nothing but questions. What would they say when they saw me? Was it really my place to be there when their son and I only had a brief relationship? The thoughts ran rampant in my head. I stood in front of that door for an eternity, uncertain what the other side had in store for me. Part of me wanted to tell his parents we were planning a future together. In reality, I was the one who needed the reassurance.

Swallowing hard, I finally placed my hand on the shiny brass knocker and quickly tapped the door. It made a loud, echoing sound I felt deep in my bones.

Frank answered the door. He was shorter than his brother, but he had the same dimpled chin and strong jawline. His hair was a shade lighter. And his eyes were deep set. They had a certain sadness to them, so different from his brother's. I saw a scar that matched James' on his left cheek. It was just as faded, but the bright sun made it appear stronger and more noticeable. His eyes were a grayer shade of blue—dark and stormy and looming in the distance ready to unleash a rainstorm.

A look of surprise filled his face as our eyes met. “You must be Helen.”

He smiled for a brief second, then turned and led me to the kitchen where his parents sat, hunched over a small wooden table, mannequins staring into a desolate street from a storefront window.

They briefly looked up and met my eyes with a slight smile, then returned to their mannequin-like state.

Frank walked me to the front door. "Thank you for stopping by. They've been locked in their own minds since they heard the news." He motioned his head towards the house. For a few seconds he remained silent, his fingers fidgeting as if reaching for the right words. "I want to hear more about your time with Jimmy, if you don't mind. It'll make things worse if we talk in front of my parents, though. Would you mind taking a ride with me? Maybe go to Ocean Drive where I can clear my head a little bit. I'll understand if you say no."

They were brothers indeed, and they both had the same love of the ocean.

"I don't mind."

After the letter he'd written, I owed it to Frank to tell him more about James' and my time together, and how happy we had been before he left. I owed it to James to help his brother through this difficult time.

We drove to Ocean Drive the very same way James and I had months before, but this time the wind was no longer wild or free. It felt stifling, like quicksand devouring anything that touched its surface. The water's waves were no longer bright, but gray and frighteningly calm.

"I think we were compatible opposites," I revealed to Frank. I couldn't think of another way to sum up the instant physical and emotional chemistry between James and me. "He was the braver version of all I wanted to be." I shrugged. "I had a desire for more in my life, but my fears always got in the way," I smiled, a little embarrassed.

"My brother has enough bravery for all of us. He was the leader, ready to take on the next adventure. I guess growing up a military brat intensified his natural inclination.

"When we moved around, he was always excited, even as a little boy. I was the complete opposite. I hated moving, and when we finally moved to Newport and stayed, it was a huge relief. I didn't have to make new friends and leave the old ones behind. I wasn't like Jimmy. He could make friends wherever he went.

"It was both his strength and his downfall. Sometimes he tried to please the wrong people and got hurt as a result of it. He constantly tried to please our father, but Dad wasn't the kind of man who could be easily pleased.

“My father worked hard and dedicated his life to the military. Without it, he was lost and miserable. The one thing that made him happy was seeing Jimmy follow in his footsteps. I guess he thought he could live vicariously through him, but it didn't last.

"He sat alone reading the paper or books on military warfare most of the time, oblivious to anyone else around him, including my mother. She tried to help him pursue other hobbies and causes, but it didn't help. He'd lost his purpose in life. It was sad to see such a proud man lose himself to melancholia. He never knew the real reason Jimmy joined.”

"To travel the world," I said rhetorically.

"You knew him quite well." He smiled at me, seemingly content to have someone else to share his experiences with. "It was good for him. Our father would finally be proud of him, and he could live out at least part of his dreams."

We walked alongside the rising waves that gently splashed the dark rocks along their path. Frank took my hand and led me to one of the giant ash-gray cliffs near the edge of the ocean. We sat there in silence for a good length of time, staring at the clear water. The clouds parted and exposed a bright sky that turned the water that exquisite shade of sapphire I loved. The silence between us didn't seem as deafening as I thought it would. My thoughts filled with memories of James, and I knew his did as well. I wasn't sure how long we sat there, surrounded by the sound of the surf and the heaviness of our hearts, but as the sky turned a bright shade of orange, we knew it was time to leave that peaceful place.

I saw Frank several times that summer. We hadn't heard any news about James' disappearance, at least not for another few weeks, but it helped having someone to talk to. Frank felt guilty for leaving his family behind while he worked in Providence. And not seeing more of his brother before he left for the war ate him up inside. I was the only other person he could talk to who knew the real James Simas.

A letter eventually came declaring James among the casualties. You can imagine how devastated we all were. His parents were heartbroken. That blank and far-away look I'd seen in their faces the day we met only intensified at the funeral.

His poor mother withdrew from the crowd and into a corner of the church. I had never seen anyone more lost. The church was filled with her deafening sobs while the priest recited prayers he must've given a hundred times throughout the war.

His father sat motionless, his head down, and hands clenched together in a tight ball. To live in a world without your child must be the deepest of hell. I couldn't imagine their pain, but I understood how tragic it was for anyone in their prime to be plucked away from the world like a worthless weed.

East Providence 2016

I felt so heartbroken hearing grandmother's story, and at

the thought of what people lost with the death of James. He had obviously been a great man who was open to the world around him. Someone who might've made a difference if only given the opportunity. I wondered what would've happened to him and my grandmother if he'd come home from the war.

Simas. I couldn't shake the thought. I dreaded asking Grandma the question, but I had to know for sure.

"Grandma, I'm a little confused. How well did you know James' brother? Am I missing something?"

A Future with Frank

We met more often as time went by. I decided to stay by Aunt Edna's until late fall. Frank and I met a few days a week to reminisce about James. It felt like the right thing to do. I wasn't ready to move back home and start my life over yet. At first, we spoke about James and how we both missed him—his carefree spirit, charismatic demeanor, and restless nature. The only thing that seemed to make both of us happy was being in each other's company, reminiscing about a man we both loved.

But even the greatest of men have their weaknesses. James had a gift for making everyone feel great in his presence. Unfortunately, he couldn't do the same for himself. He was always looking for something he couldn't quite find.

The more I spent time with Frank, the fonder of him I grew. At first sight, he wasn't as charismatic as his brother. He didn't try to charm everyone he met with a smile or a flattering word, but he was comfortable in his own skin—something that was charming in and of itself.

He was a noble man who had an immense love for his family. He moved back home to help his parents overcome their grief, even though they were too caught up in their own darkness to help him with his. He'd stood enveloped in the shadow of his older brother his entire life, but he never resented James for a moment. Instead, he quietly took his place in the family and channeled that energy into making the most out of his life.

After weeks of getting along so well, there was a change in

Frank. He looked away when I spoke to him, almost afraid to meet my glance, and he would find excuses to make our visits short. He was trying to push me away, but I didn't understand why. The hurt surprised me, and I had to see him again to find out what I'd done wrong. With little thought, I decided to go to Ocean Drive, hoping to find him there.

As I expected, Frank sat on one of the rocks, staring out at the water. He rubbed his forehead in heavy strokes, his hands fidgeting as they did when he felt uneasy. I walked over to him, placing one foot in front of another on the jagged edge of the rocks, trying not to lose my balance. The wind was powerful and the water just as agitated. I remember my heart beating faster as I approached him, worried he would tell me we couldn't see each other again.

I touched his shoulder as I moved closer. He turned his head toward me, and then jerked his body back.

"What are you doing here? His eyes were red, sweat running down his forehead in beads.

"Why are you ignoring me? What did I do wrong?"

"I needed some time to think."

"About what? You can trust me, you know. I thought we were getting along well." My heart beat faster and my mind raced, trying to understand where things had gone wrong.

"That's exactly why. Don’t you see!"

It was the first time I'd heard panic and anger in his voice.

"See what?" Tears welled in my eyes.

He stood up from the rock and looked into my eyes, his face softening. He grabbed my hand and dropped it a second later, as if a hot coal burned his skin. Afraid to face me, he turned away. I started to leave, feeling defeated and lost for the second time in my life since James' death.

"Helen, wait!" His face softened again. "Please come back."

I stopped in my tracks. I didn't know what to do. Maybe it was best to let things go. I wasn't sure. As I turned to look at him, his eyes reflected the same sadness I'd seen the first time we met. I knew, then, that I had to stay.

He took my hand, but this time he didn't let go. With his other hand, he touched my cheek and smiled. I couldn't help but smile back. I placed my hand on his, and it felt surprisingly natural. He came closer slowly and kissed me. I didn't resist. I couldn't because it was right.

"I love you, Helen. It's crazy, but I can't see my life without you. My brother is probably turning in his grave right now! What kind of man falls in love with his brother's girl? What kind of man am I?" He let go, backed away, raising his hands in the air, as if waiting for an answer from the heavens above.

I had no words. I hadn't realized things had changed between us somewhere along the way, but there was no denying now that they had. Somehow, I'd misinterpreted his secret glances and the adrenaline coursing through me each time we held hands to steady our steps upon those slippery cliffs.

There was a reason I couldn't walk away from him when

he tried to push me away. What kind of woman falls in love with her guy's brother? Could it be so wrong, if it were true?

"A good man whom I've shared sorrow and happiness with. I don't regret any of the time we've spent together," I called out.

He slowly walked back and took my hands in his. He gazed into my eyes. I tried to find the sadness in his eyes that had become as familiar to me as my own reflection, but it wasn't there. My own happiness was the only thing that reflected back at me. He moved closer and placed his lips on mine once more. It was in that moment that I realized I had fallen in love again. But this time it was for good.

East Providence 2016

"If you're asking me if Frank is your grandfather, the answer is yes."

. I was dumbfounded. The person who I'd trusted my entire life had hidden James, my granduncle, from me—and one of the most important parts of her life - after I poured out my soul to her time and time again.

"Was I the only one who didn't know?" I swallowed hard hoping to get rid of the disappointment creeping up my throat.

The woman I had admired for so long had a secret life I'd never known about.

"Quite the contrary, my dear. You are the only one who knows besides your late grandfather. I hope I haven't disappointed you too much." She smiled confidently.

"I understand that you're upset, but no one's life is perfect. We all have a past. Your grandfather and I both struggled with guilt during our relationship. We hadn't a clue whether we were doing the right thing for our families or for James. But, together, we were whole for the first time in our lives. You have to remember that as I got to know your grandfather, his remarkable traits shone through each day. He was compassionate, gentle, and loving—an extraordinary human being that would never harm another soul. How could I not fall in love with him?

“Sometimes our greatest loss in life turns out to be our greatest blessing. I was blessed to have known your granduncle James and to have made wonderful memories with him, but because of him, I met the man who became my lifelong partner. Frank was an outstanding husband and father the entire time we were married. Of course, we had our disagreements as any couple does, but the one constant was the love we shared for each other. I will miss him and cherish his memory until my dying breath."

Conflicting thoughts ran rampant through my head. I was crushed that my grandmother hadn't confided in me before that moment, like I had with her so many times. But did I really have the right to know everything about her? She had a life before her family. Before me. And only she could decide what parts of it to share and what parts to hide beneath the surface.

"I didn't tell you the truth because it was not the time or place. Something like this is sometimes seen as taboo, but it's not right to ignore or abandon what or whom you love because someone else thinks it's wrong. I lived a blissful life with your grandfather. If I had given into what others thought or said, I would've regretted it every day of my life."

My grandma was the only person who favored feelings over truth and love over social obligation. While everyone preached the importance of truth while I was a growing up, only she realized that sometimes the truth hurt worse than any lie, even with the best intentions.

I sighed, realizing she had indeed lived up to her reputation, it seemed.

"I think I understand why you did what you did. Thank you for telling me."

"You've always reminded me of my younger self, Rebecca. We both think with our hearts instead of our minds. I hope you never regret that or put yourself down for it." She gave me one of her reassuring smiles.

When it came to doing the right thing, I *always* thought she put too much faith in me, but it was especially true this time.

Part II

CHAPTER SIX

It was the first night I hadn't dreamed of either one of them. Instead, I wandered around my grandmother's garden at the age of six, picking vegetables. It was a sunny August afternoon. The warm rays of sunlight touched my forehead, and my long ponytail danced in anticipation. I wore my favorite yellow-daisy romper that day because it matched the yellow daisies blooming in abundance in Grandma's garden. I ran through the side door, zigzagging through the hallway, finally stopping in the kitchen. I caught a glimpse of her profile over the counter, hovering over the dough she carefully kneaded between her hands.

Her shoulder-length hair was pulled back in a high bun, generously sprinkled with long strands of silver. She smiled as soon as she turned and saw me running toward her. Her eyes were bright, adorned with small creases that reminded me of the plump folds in the heirloom tomatoes in her garden. I stood on my tippy toes eagerly spying over the counter, hoping to get a glimpse of what she was baking. She gently patted the tip of my nose.

The scene gently slipped away, and in its place a blinding streak of sun peeked through the white-laced curtains in the bedroom. With that, reality replaced fantasy. I was lying down in the same bed I'd slept in many times while visiting Grandma's house as a young girl. She left it the same way year after year. The pink lace comforter, the matching curtains, and the big white teddy bear with a fire-engine red bow gently tied around his neck—they were all there, exactly as I left them over twenty years ago. In her eyes it was my room. My younger sister, Colleen, had her own room there too, and the hand-painted unicorns still graced the lilac walls.

On the weekends, my parents had often dropped us off at

Grandma's house while they enjoyed the sights and sounds of downtown Providence. Grandma always greeted me in the same way—with a hug and a kiss on the forehead—up until the day I left for college.

I couldn't help thinking about our conversation the night before. My grandmother consistently knew the right decision to make, and because of that, she'd made a wonderful life for herself. Even though she saw herself in me, I didn't have her strength. Still, my greatest wish had always been to be like her when I grew up. She was confident, beautiful, and knew how to fix things, whether they were petty, immaterial things or complicated human emotions.

Bzzzz. I reached over to glance at my phone, knowing instantly who had sent the text. *"Hey, hope you're enjoying your trip. Just want to tell you that I miss you.*

I threw the phone on the bed and headed to the main bathroom for a hot shower.

As I breathed the warm steam in, my mind began to clear.

The anxiety that had crept into my body melted away with each gentle tickle of the water droplets hitting my skin. My thoughts floated away with the steam.

After a few minutes, the water grew cooler, awakening me from the peaceful trance, and I headed back to the bedroom and stared at the text, my hair still dripping wet. The tightly wrapped towel around my body did little to keep me from shivering. However, it wasn't from the cold, but from my nervousness as the message stared back at me. For the first time, I didn't know how to respond.

I left my home in Providence for something more years ago. Something that would calm the restlessness deep within my bones. I thought I'd found it in another state. And in Robert. He was the man I'd always hoped to find—someone who wasn't only handsome, but a true partner who would offer me an escape from an ordinary life. I wanted to be surrounded by nice things and great opportunities. Wasn't that something everyone secretly dreamed of, even if they were too embarrassed to admit it? I wanted the opportunity to travel the world and to build a lifetime of memories with someone who would look at me the same way my grandfather looked at my grandmother when they thought no one was looking.

I was sure I'd found it—almost sure—until I no longer was. And I couldn't stop the sinking feeling that I was in the wrong place, yet again.

Robert was the owner of a region-wide jewelry business that had started two generations ago with his grandfather Roberto Nastasi, an Italian immigrant from Monforte San Giorgio—a small village deep in the hills, thirty-nine kilometers from Messina, Sicily. I'd visited the village once with Robert during early summer. It was a delightful, quaint town with winding cobblestone paths and crumbling stone arches. Each *via* revealed hidden paths left unchanged for over seventy years.

The stone houses were adorned with pastel shutters and ornate iron balconies. In the distance, they became one with the landscape, reminding me of godlike figures carved into blocks of marble thousands of years ago. The area gleamed with historical charm. Its most notable landmark was the elaborate Byzantine monastery, dating back to the eighth and nineth centuries. Its paths made time stand still, and its rolling hills created a breathtaking vista of lush valleys that stretched to the brilliant blue horizon before disappearing miles into the distance.

We started dating three years ago after meeting at a coworker's dinner party on New Year's Eve. I'd noticed him from across the room, speaking to a few of the senior members of our sales team. He held a drink in one hand and motioned to something with his left. It seemed he was pitching an idea to the group, and the guys all nodded in agreement. He stopped for a moment, then let out a strong laugh. The rest of the group roared with laughter as they each patted his back and walked away.

He stood alone for a moment scanning the room, slowly swirling his drink. I studied his features in admiration. His dark almond-shaped eyes shined with excitement. Thick, dark eyebrows perfectly framed them, emphasizing their natural sparkle. As he caught sight of a familiar face, he motioned them to him with a magnetic smile that was contagious to everyone nearby. The sole patch under his lower lip, and five o'clock shadow completed the rugged, masculine look that was hard for any woman to resist.

As soon as his gaze turned my direction, I couldn't help but look away, a bit embarrassed that I had been caught red-handed in my admiration. I peered his way again, and as we briefly caught each other's glance, my cheeks warmed. Before I knew it, a middle-aged senior executive had led him into another business conversation.

I spent the rest of the evening chatting with coworkers, all the while scanning the room for the guy who could transform a previously strong and independent woman in her early thirties into a hopeless schoolgirl.

I lost sight of him for a few minutes, and just like that bright-eyed schoolgirl, I was crushed. I had almost given up hope until I turned and saw him standing behind me. I froze, unable to make a sound.

"Hi." He flashed a flirtatious smile.

After a few awkward seconds, I managed to pry the word

"hi" from my lips, but not before getting a second rush of blood to my cheeks. "Sorry, you startled me," I said, trying to recover.

"I didn't mean to scare you. I noticed you from across the room a few times, and thought I'd introduce myself—Robert Nastasi." He put out his hand and smiled that radiant smile that soon became my kryptonite.

"I don't scare easily," I replied with a smile of my own. The strong, independent woman found herself after a second or two. I gave him my hand, but I could sense the schoolgirl returning, as his hand gently squeezed mine, lingering for a bit longer than he should have.

He offered me a drink, and before long, we were talking about his family and business. He told me how proud he was to carry on his family tradition. Both his grandfather and father had worked to build a successful company from the ground up, with little money and growing families to support. Robert was now responsible for continuing the legacy and making it as successful as possible. He considered it both a gift and a curse at times, but it was now part of the man he'd become.

We hadn't spoken much about my plans or goals, even though I'd managed to move up the ranks to the role of art director in only two years, but I never liked talking about my own accomplishments anyway.

Looking back, it probably should have been my cue to stop the relationship before it started. If it had been any other time or any other guy, I would've ended the conversation then and there. But Robert wasn't any other guy, and he wasn't one I could easily forget. His smile had a way of distracting my thoughts and getting under my skin, like a river rushing through my veins.

As the night progressed, the rhythmic jazz playing in the background slowed to a crooning melody. Robert asked me to dance, and as we moved across the floor, laughing and flirting, he pulled me closer with every spin. Before I knew it, our host began the countdown to the New Year. We stopped dancing and glanced at each other. I didn't know whether he would stay—as I hoped he would—or excuse himself to find a date he had neglected too long.

Instead of leaving, he leaned toward me and kissed my lips at the stroke of midnight. Their warmth lingered, like the sweet scent of rain on a warm spring day. I yearned for them as soon as he pulled away. My lips were lost without his. I was hooked like I had never been before.

That moment seemed so far away now. I still loved Robert. My heart still searched for him when he was far. And his kisses still seduced me from reality. I had a great life with him in New York City, but there was always something missing. His success allowed me to travel around the world, to meet interesting and important people in society, but the missing pieces floated around us, keeping me from feeling whole. I had everything I needed, but I still felt alone. Robert's needs and those of his business seemed to come before mine every time.

After the argument we'd had several weeks ago, I had to find the strength to make changes. I was stuck in limbo, unable to move forward. I began questioning all of the decisions I'd made during the last decade of my life. My job. My move to New York. And my relationship with Robert.

Did I make a big mistake by moving from Providence so long ago?

CHAPTER SEVEN

I had plans to drive grandmother to the doctor's office later in the day. The sun was out, and the light gusts of wind made it the perfect New England summer afternoon. Grandma enjoyed days like these. She regularly made sure to take a stroll for the sole purpose of feeling the warmth of the sun on her skin. When Grandpa was alive, the two of them took walks together, enjoying each other's company as they had for most of their married life. Once he had passed, Grandma continued her walks as a way of remembering her husband, knowing he would always be with her in spirit.

The last few years, her legs had stopped working the way

they used to, but she still made the effort to enjoy what she loved. At times, I would catch resentment in her voice, when her body fought back with the pain of old age. She longed for the carefree days of her youth, when she could be outdoors without limitations, and spoke of them often. Her body worked in unison with her mind back then. Now, it betrayed her, like everyone's body did when they were lucky enough to grow old. It kept her at home more than she wanted and slowed down her pace.

Her mind remained sharp, however. Over the years, she realized the only way to remain happy was to accept it, and to make the most of what she *could* do. She relied on her memories and her music. When her body didn't cooperate, she sat in her living room and played the records she prized so dearly. She would watch them spin on the gramophone, the scratch of static bringing with it each memory that had been safely tucked away in her mind, like a priceless relic encased in delicate museum glass.

"They bring me back to some of the greatest moments I had in my life," she would explain, as I sat there curiously watching a faint smile appear on her face. "Music can do what nothing else can."

I shook my head, chasing the thoughts away, and quickly picked up my purse from the dresser. "Grandma, are you ready? We can catch some lunch after your appointment," I shouted while sifting through my purse for the car keys, hoping she could hear me from the other side of the house.

"I've been waiting for *you,* my dear," she replied with a smile, as she appeared in front of my bedroom door only seconds later.

I couldn't help but smile. For an old lady, she still had impeccable timing.

CHAPTER EIGHT

We went to a trendy lunch spot in downtown Providence—Downcity—as the locals called it, Grandma reminded me. It had been years since I'd left Providence, but my grandmother had become somewhat of a native after she and my grandfather permanently moved close to the area when they married over seventy years ago.

They lived a happy life, from what I could tell as a child. They laughed often and took long walks after Sunday dinners, all while holding hands. I often saw my grandmother wrap herself around my grandfather's right arm, bringing him close. He would turn to her with a smile and return the gesture with a loving kiss on her cheek. They trailed behind me while I ran off exploring the wooded area behind their little Cape Cod home in East Providence. I remember the excitement of running through those trees and pretending to scavenge the trails for hidden treasures. I would shake my head and laugh, leaving little Colleen behind as she desperately tried to keep up with me.

"Rebecca? You haven't told me what's been bothering you. All my secrets are out now. I think it's time you told me yours." Grandma picked up her glass and drank the warm tea, a look of confidence crossed her face, knowing she could extract a confession in the same way she so easily had when I was young.

"I don't really have any secrets. Things have gotten complicated, that's all." I looked away, worried that my missing poker face would give away my thoughts.

"I thought you were happy with Robert. He's what you always wanted, isn't he? What's missing?"

"Something I never realized until I ran into an old friend."

I landed in Providence only a week before to visit my grandmother while Robert stayed home working on details for his newest grand opening. I was a little disappointed, but it hadn't been the first time. Each time business picked up, I would see less and less of him. I kept myself busy when he was gone, staying at work longer or attending some boring happy-hour work function—excuses not to sit at home in an empty apartment. I'd hoped he would trust me enough to talk about the family business, even if only to ask my opinion on an advertising campaign. But every time I asked about a new opening or product line, Robert would mutter the same words, "everything's good, nothing to worry about."

After hearing those words too many times, I needed to get away. After all, traveling by myself would help clear my head. It had been a while since I'd seen my grandmother, and visiting her had always made me feel better, so I headed back to Providence.

I stopped at my old neighborhood to visit my parents first. They were enjoying their new lives as empty nesters in a small condo a few minutes from my childhood home. They loved the unexpected visits that they'd grown to expect from me over the years.

After eating a ton of food that my mother put out for me and answering a dozen questions from my father about my adventures in New York, I headed out to one of my favorite parks, Hunts Mills Trails.

I'd discovered the spot my sophomore year of high school when Kent took me there during the summer. He was the only guy I knew who preferred the outdoors to the annoying drama-ridden house parties our classmates threw. We had lots of fun together without the complication of a relationship. It was too comfortable to be anything more than a friendship. When I left for college, I had to leave that behind with the rest of my life in Providence. On occasion, I'd think about the great times we had together. He was a good guy and I hoped he was as happy as I thought I'd be in New York.

The adjustment to my new home hadn't been too difficult, but every time I passed Central Park and spotted people hiking the trails, part of me ached to go back to when all I needed was nature and Kent by my side. I quickly pushed those thoughts behind me, however, and reminded myself of the more practical path I had committed myself to. Soon enough, those happy memories faded into the distance as the hectic city lifestyle consumed my days and nights.

The Red Blaze Trail was my favorite trail in Hunts Mill. Surrounded by rocks, shrubs, and blooming mountain laurel in midsummer, it was a passageway to a different time. The stone-step edge led to a path that meandered into the depths of a dense forest, hidden from the rest of the world around it. The trail opened up to the peaceful waterways of Ten Mile River and Turner Reservoir. I easily lost myself within its beauty, just as other locals had a hundred years before. The historic John Hunt House stood tall and prominent in its eggshell-yellow paint among the greenery and river falls surrounding it.

My heartbeat quickened as I drove into the parking lot, seeing the trail head in front of me. The scent of the trees and blooming wildflowers infused my nostrils with their sweet and earthy scent. The birds chirped high above the treetops in a symphonic arrangement that awakened my senses. I couldn't help but smile as memories flooded my mind, and at that moment, I couldn't remember why I had ever decided to leave.

As I headed towards the start of the trail, I notice the sound of children's voices and laughter coming from the left. The voices were followed by a male voice that sounded somewhat familiar to me, like an old song that hadn't played in years but whose tune brought on a strange sense of Déjà vu.

"You guys slow down a bit," the male voice called out in between breaths.

I turned my head in the direction of the voice and saw a man in his thirties dressed in jeans, a blue and white plaid shirt, and a worn Nirvana cap. I couldn't get a good look at him, but he was tall and muscular, a short, neatly trimmed beard shaping his long, thin face. His appearance didn't belong to anyone I could remember.

He turned towards me at the clinking of my keys as they fell to the ground, missing the shallow pockets of my shorts. He stopped and stared without a word.

"Rebecca?" he said in a slight whisper, remaining motionless for a few seconds, as if he'd caught sight of a doe in her natural habitat.

"Yes?" I stopped, curious to find out whose face I had erased from my memory too early.

"It's Kent Wilding. We went to high school together—East Providence."

"Kent! I didn't recognize you. You…you look so different."

"I know. The beard and the two kids." He smirked.

His quick wit definitely hadn't changed. His two boys stopped in their tracks, eager to learn who I was. Kent motioned them to continue their game of exploration farther along the path, but within eyesight.

"You look good." He stared for a brief moment, but not brief enough before my cheeks began to flush.

I quickly tried to make small talk, hoping he hadn't noticed.

"So do you. Are you still living in East Providence?"

"I am. I'm an English teacher at Riverside Middle School."

I hadn't pictured him as a teacher. A journalist, maybe. But not a teacher. I thought he'd turn out to be a famous novelist. His first love was writing, and his close second was the outdoors. I had admired how confident he was in everything he did. He never worried about what other classmates thought of him, and he never tried to impress anyone in order to be liked. It was an ability I couldn't grasp no matter how hard I'd tried back then. I'd repeatedly tried to impress the wrong people, and I was never really happy outside of my time with Kent. My only drive had been to leave.

"I never pursued writing, if that's what you're thinking."

After all this time, he still managed to read my thoughts. In school, he was the one I could always confide in. And he always seemed to know when I needed him most. He listened to my heartbreaks and complaints about the popular friends I'd lost because I couldn't fake an interest in the stupid things they liked.

Kent was the only one who understood my need to stay home with my sketchpad because he did the same thing with his notebook.

I remembered the short stories and poetry he wrote. He would sit down for only a few minutes before his immense creativity poured out of his pen, flooding his notebook with beautiful, meaningful tales. I'd never seen anyone so dedicated before.

When Kent and I didn't hike together, we hung out at the local coffeehouse. He would jot things down in that little notebook he carried hidden in the pocket of his charcoal gray hoodie, lined in blue and gray plaid. No one else knew it was there, except me. I would complain about the annoying cheerleaders in my homeroom, and he would create a hilarious story about them to make me laugh.

"Give me 15 minutes," he would say.

I would go back to the coffee counter for a refill, and he would create a whole plot in a matter of minutes.

He had so much more substance than any of the students in

our school who circulated meaningless gossip as part of their daily routine. I could rely on him to not sugarcoat things, especially when it came to guys. He always told me not to worry about the loser guy who didn't give me the time of day.

"He's not worth your time," he would say. "There's someone else out there that will appreciate you."

Somehow those words made it all better.

At times, I would catch him quietly contemplating, his left eyebrow arched, and his lips tightly pursed together, as if trying to hold back the words from his mouth. In those moments, he drifted away from reality, temporarily locked in his own mind, carefully observing some bystander who sparked his creativity. In the blink of an eye, he would return from that sweet internal prison, like a bird set free from his cage, jot some notes down, and make a witty comment. I often got his attention during those deep thoughts by asking, "Genius at work?" as I secretly looked forward to reading his next creation.

"But why? You were so good at it." I couldn't contain my

disappointment at finding out that he had abandoned his talent.

"As cliché as it sounds, life got in the way. I lost my inspiration years ago." He smiled a melancholy smile of defeat. "How about we meet up for coffee for old time sakes? No kids this time."

I couldn't think of a reason not to. "I'd love to," I said with a smile.

CHAPTER NINE

I got to the Coffee Exchange about five minutes early. The outside looked about the same, a newer version of the green and brown historic building I remembered. It was a common sight on Wickenden Street, to see many of the historic buildings impeccably restored, and no doubt, part of its enduring charm. The interior of my favorite coffee shop was now trendier, with fancy coffee-drink names like *affogato*, *cold brew*, and *flat white* listed on their large chalkboards—much different than what I remembered from frequenting it years ago. Millennials and college students replaced the grungy kids who sat at the tables in their backward hats, plaid flannel shirts, and Doc Marten boots.

I sat down at a small round marble-top table speckled with brown and black. I smiled as I looked over at a couple sitting to my right, engrossed in a competitive game of chess. Kent and I used to sit at that very same table fifteen years ago. He scrunched over his notebook writing while I sketched pictures of trees and old houses I'd seen in town. It was the only time I felt centered, the restlessness melting away like snow under the April sun.

I glanced away from the table and my distant high school memory, and suddenly, in front of me, stood Kent. He was standing there smiling, knowing exactly where my mind had taken me.

"I see you found our table," he said.

His blue eyes were still the same shade of sapphire I'd adored, but now they were adorned with small, fine lines. I managed to hide my admiration of them in our youth, except once, when I blurted out "you have nice eyes" for no apparent reason.

Kent had blushed for the first time in front of me, but as usual, he recovered with a sarcastic remark. Any other girl would've melted from his warm gaze. Unfortunately, I never did. Perhaps because I had never truly seen them before that moment.

He stood in front of me now—a different person—a full-grown man whose clean-cut hair replaced the floppy-haired teenager I remembered spending time with. He'd grown into an attractive man whose eyes were still as tender as I remembered.

"I thought it would be nice to walk down memory lane for a bit," I said recovering from my thoughts.

"Are you going to tell me how nice my eyes are again?" He let out a chuckle that lit up his face.

"I can't believe you remember that!" I looked away, too embarrassed to face him.

"I'm sorry. I didn't mean to make fun of you." His face straightened and his tone grew more solemn. "I remember a lot about you, actually."

He reached across the table and touched my hand, then looked deep into my eyes, something he'd avoided when we were younger. "I thought about you a lot after you left. All the things I wanted to tell you, but couldn't. I wrote them down and hid them away for safekeeping. Sometimes to forget. Sometimes to revisit the memories.

"I read them on the nights I couldn't sleep. Maybe in hopes of dreaming about you one more time. For years, I thought about what would've happened if I'd shown them to you. If anything would've changed for us."

He stopped and looked down, obviously now aware that the words that had spilled from his lips had been said out loud. "I'm sorry."

"Don't be. I'm sorry I never realized it. I was selfishly thinking about myself and not noticing anything going on around me." I sighed in disappointment and stared at his hand on mine, wondering why I had missed the signs.

"No, you weren't. I just couldn't be honest with you like I should've. But I have to be honest with you now that I have the opportunity. Do you remember homecoming junior year?"

“I do. Our dates both stood us up.” I shook my head, remembering how disappointed I had been.

“You helped me get out of a rut when I found out my date ditched me for some lame jock. So no, you were never selfish.”

“It probably wasn't the best decision to go out on a trail late at night in fancy clothes though.” I couldn’t help but laugh as the moment came back to me.

“It's one of my favorite memories. I had never seen anyone more stunning than you that night.”

I blushed at the compliment, remembering how fun that night had turned out as we lay down on the ground watching the twinkling stars. I had never seen the sky so dark, but it didn’t feel threatening or scary. Not with Kent by my side.

He let go of my hand. “I’m sorry, but I have to get going. I'm teaching summer classes, and I have to be there in thirty minutes. I'd like to see you again if you're still in town. Maybe we can meet back at the trail Wednesday morning at ten. If you want. I’d understand if it’s too weird now.” He looked down, his cheeks reddening.

"No, I don’t mind. It would be nice. Can you show me what you wrote? If you'd don't mind, of course." As soon as the words left my mouth, I felt horrible for asking. After being away for so long, I knew I had no right to ask, but somehow, I needed to know what I'd left behind.

"I can do that. I only have myself to blame for bringing it up, right? I always had a hard time saying no to you." He smiled and rose from his seat, brushing my arm with his hand as he left.

I sat in my chair a few minutes longer, reminiscing about Kent. How amazing it would be to go back in time and fix the mistakes I'd made. I made a few, especially when it came to him. I snapped out of my nostalgia when a customer asked if I was using the vacant chair at my table. Shaking my head, I got up from my seat. It was time to head back to my grandmother's.

The sun shone through the cloudless sky, warming my shoulders as I headed out to Hunts Mills Trail again. I passed several new shops and buildings along the way, but some of the old ones remained proud and tall, monuments to a time I'd tried so hard to forget. It was all coming back to me now.

I hadn't been able to get my mind off Kent the last few days, and today wasn't any different. I looked forward to seeing him again. It was a strange feeling. I wanted to go back and change things between us. I had missed his clues while focusing on a future I thought was right for me instead of being fully in the moment. And it had blinded me to who Kent really was. Who he could've been for me.

Although everyone had pointed out what a nice couple we would make, I never saw it. Maybe my stubbornness or natural inclination to do the opposite of what I was told did me in.

But we couldn't go back, could we? Or was this an opportunity to change things and make them right?

He had grown into a handsome man who hadn't lost the

inner qualities I admired most. It made me feel shallow. The reason I hadn't been attracted to Kent in the first place was the exact reason I found him attractive now.

Where did that leave Robert? I still loved him, but maybe his outside blinded me from seeing what he was on the inside.

So far, my trip brought up more questions than it did answers. I thought about the lunch I'd had with my grandmother a few days before, and imagined what she would say about me meeting Kent again.

I parked my car and hurried to the trail. The cloudless sky made the lush green of the giant trees brighter. It felt comforting, just like it used to. I sat down on the stone steps at the beginning of the trail, waiting. My mind drifted to the days I'd hiked those trails and enjoyed the company of those very trees.

Back then, when Kent joined me, he had been more prepared than me with snacks, bug spray, pocketknives, and fire starters in his pack. I, on the other hand, had the proper clothing and shoes, water, and my sketchpad. Nothing more.

When we had taken food and water breaks, I'd linger longer when inspired to sketch. Kent never complained and waited patiently, daydreaming away among the mesmerizing surroundings. A few times, I caught him staring as I drew. He always denied anything other than enjoying my concentrating expression—the biting of my lower lip and the squinting of my eyes. He would quickly brush the topic off and change the subject.

"Hi."

I was brought out of the memory by Kent's voice.

"I hope you weren't waiting long."

"No, I wasn't."

I smiled oblivious to the passing of time since I'd arrived. It might've been a few minutes or maybe half an hour.

I got up, and we started walking. We walked in silence for a while, listening to the sound of the birds and crickets and the buzzing of bees who eagerly flew alongside us. It was like old times. We'd often walked in silence then, until Kent broke the ice with news about the latest story he was working on. This time it was different, though. He turned to look at me with nothing but a smile. I had to start the conversation.

"Do you still come here regularly?" I asked.

"I try to, at least once a week, maybe more. Before kids, I used to get out here four times a week. It gave me time to reflect on stuff. He hesitated for a minute, and then blurted out, "Are you happy in New York?"

"I was. I thought it was what I wanted—to start a new life somewhere else, somewhere with more possibilities. You can't get more *big city* than the Big Apple."

"Was it really that bad here?" His voice cracked, and his eyes grew darker as he looked toward me.

"It wasn't. Really!" I immediately regretted how my comment might've made him feel. "I don't know why I had to leave. Providence never felt like home for some reason, but I don't know anymore. It might've been a mistake all along. Have you been happy here?"

"This was always home, but I haven't always been happy. Eventually, I was. I still thought about you a lot after you left. I missed our time together." He reached into his pocket and drew out a note that looked like it had been folded and refolded countless times. Without a word he handed it to me.

I feel you in the swaying trees, the trickle of the morning rain,

Your voice, gliding along the wind's gentle breath.

In my mind and soul,

I live for the moment my eyes awake to find you near.

What I'd give to feel your skin beneath my fingertips,

To lose myself in the dark pools of your eyes.

To kiss your sweet lips would change my darkness

To a wondrous morning light,

Bright, pure, and rich with hope.

My only wish is to spend my days beside you,

To find a perfect solace that only your arms can hold.

I stared at the poem, speechless. His amorous words tore like blades through my heart. I'd never realized the depth of his feelings. I walked away from a great man who loved me regardless of my faults, doubts, and insecurities. I was his inspiration and his misery. In that moment, I hated myself.

"I fell in love with you the first time I saw you walking through the door of science class." He let out a long sigh. "You walked into the room, wide-eyed with those beautiful brown eyes and long dark hair tucked behind your ears. You always tucked your hair when you were nervous.

"The more time I spent with you, the more I wanted to make you laugh and smile. Your face would light up, and your eyes would sparkle at my lame jokes".

He chuckled at the memory, and then a trace of misery

filled his voice. "All the while, I hoped you would somehow read those emotions in my eyes, in my words, or even when I silently watched you sketching. I was too stupid and too scared to tell you how I felt. For a kid who was good with words, I just couldn't say them out loud to you. I meant to give you the poem the day you left. It was the only way I knew to explain my feelings. It was my last chance, but you were so excited to start your adventure…

"I couldn't ruin it for you, even if I had the slimmest chance of changing your mind. It was too farfetched. When I saw you again, everything came rushing back. I was that lame kid who wasn't brave enough to tell you I loved you."

I felt broken, a glass dropped from a skyscraper whose pieces shattered aimlessly across the road.

"I'm so sorry." I shook my head in self-disgust. I couldn't believe I'd been so blind of the one person who had been there for me completely. It had become a habit of mine, to miss out on what was right in front of me. I had chosen Robert—someone who had me questioning his feelings for me—over a man who continued loving me for years.

I looked at his gentle eyes and a memory came back, a bolt of lightning in the quiet midnight sky. Kent had indeed tried to reveal his feelings, and in one climatic moment, he'd tried to kiss me. I couldn't believe I had locked that memory far within the recesses of my mind until now. It flooded back in detail.

A few months before I left for college, Kent and I went to the movies together. After the show, he'd insisted on walking me to my car, even though he never had before. We talked about the movie we'd seen, and I joked, half serious, that he would've written a better screenplay if given the chance. He gave me the same half-smile he gave every time I paid him a compliment.

Standing in front of me, hands shoved in his pockets, he nervously kicked the tiny gravel pebbles, making a crackling sound that mimicked the heavy chirping of crickets. I fumbled through my purse for my keys and smiled at him. With a slight hesitation, he moved closer, his eyes closing and his lips heading toward mine. I tensed in surprise, and arched the opposite way. He opened his eyes for a second, noticing my reaction, then quickly turned and headed the other way without a word.

We never spoke about what happened that night, even though we'd had countless chances before I left. It was as if nothing happened, as if it were a meaningless scene deleted from a movie.

"Do you remember that night at the movies?" I asked. "I wonder what would've happened if I'd let you kiss me." I caught myself saying out loud.

"I remember. It doesn’t matter now." He looked down, kicking the tiny pebbles that lay in front of his feet like he had that night. I could see the younger version of him in spite of his changed appearance. He was the sarcastic artist and dreamer I'd always known him to be.

"Can we go back for just a moment?" I asked.

Without a word, he leaned toward me the same way he had long ago. I stood still in anticipation, free from hesitation. I could hear the sound of my own breath quickening as he got closer. His lips gently brushed mine at first, the flutter of a butterfly's wings teasing a flower as it gently landed on its delicate petals. As his lips entwined with mine, his breath flowed throughout my body.

Cruelly, my mind wandered to imaginary memories that we could've had together. It was a book whose story was left unread, forever suspended by what ifs. We might've had a remarkable life together, holding hands often as our kids and then grandkids ran ahead of us into a tree-lined path. It was something I would never find out unless….

"You don't know how long I've waited for that." A faint smile appeared on his face as he touched my cheek. "I'm sorry, but I can't stay. I really wish I didn't have to leave."

My heart sank, realizing it *was* too late. "I guess the dream was better than the real thing, then," I murmured under my breath, realizing he didn't feel the way I'd hoped he did.

"Are you kidding me? It was exactly what I thought it would be." His eyes softened, but that gorgeous shade of blue couldn't hide a trace of sadness. "It's eight years too late." He paused. "I'm married."

I was breathless in the worst possible way. Of course, that explained the kids with him the other day, but I hadn't noticed a ring. I had made things more complicated for both of us now. That forbidden kiss proved how Kent felt about me, but it didn't give me any answers. Like a puzzle without any clues, it confused me more than ever, filling my head with thoughts and emotions I didn't know existed. My life could've been different if only I had let him kiss me that night.

"I'm sorry I asked you to kiss me. I should've guessed."

"You didn't make me do anything I didn't want to do so many times before." He touched my cheek with his hand, and briefly looked into my eyes. I thought he would kiss me once more, but he slowly looked away instead.

"We can forget the whole thing happened." The words burned as they poured from my lips.

"I don't want to forget it. When you left, I thought about what our lives could've been like together…if I'd been brave enough to stop you from leaving. I thought about you every morning I awoke and every night as I drifted off to sleep. Eventually, I met someone who fell in love with me, but somehow, I never forgot you completely."

"Did you love her?" A hint of jealousy eased into my chest, something I had no right to feel.

"I did. I do, but it's complicated. We've grown apart over the years, and it's my fault. I never really let her into my heart, not the way she deserves, and I think she finally realized it." He reached for my hand and held it for a minute, then dropped it, as if a rage of guilt thundered through him like a dark, lingering cloud.

"I understand what you mean. Funny how life works out that way, isn't it? There's a guy I would do anything for, but I don't know if he would do the same for me."

"You deserve a lot more than that, Rebecca. Don't settle." His brow clenched with disapproval.

"I don't deserve you, do I? Is it too late for us, then?" I asked, not realizing I had said the words out loud.

"I wish I could tell you it wasn't. I can't tell you how much I want to touch you, to hold you in my arms and show you how much I love you. But I'm married to wonderful woman who has created a family with me. We have our differences, but I can't leave her. I can't betray her like that, even though my mind and heart betrayed her every time I thought about you. She's a good woman. Her only mistake was falling in love with a man who couldn't love her the same way. And my boys—it would devastate them."

I realized right then and there what I had gained and lost in a matter of minutes. Kent was the same decent and caring guy I'd met in high school. He would never hurt anyone intentionally, so it was only fitting that he would never break up his marriage or his family—not even for the woman he had secretly loved most of his life. He wouldn't leave her for me, and I understood, even though it broke my heart.

"Do you regret the kiss?" I asked meekly, afraid to hear his answer.

"Not for a minute."

"I wish things were different, but then you wouldn't be you. Please be happy." I touched his cheek and looked at him, trying to engrain his face deep into my memory.

I never wanted to forget the way his sapphire eyes looked at me. He placed his hand on mine and kissed my cheek. He cradled my face between his hands and placed his forehead on mine, as if trying to take in every breath of my being before we parted forever.

"I'll try. There are different forms of happiness. You've always been my muse, and I think you've inspired me again. I won't forget you, ever. No matter what. Promise me you'll allow yourself to be happy."

I nodded in agreement, but clenched his hand one last time, hoping I could freeze time for a moment longer. He brought me into his arms and wiped the tears that trailed down my cheeks, then let go.

I left without looking back.

CHAPTER TEN

On the drive back, I cried like I never had before. Instead of finding answers, I'd made things hazier. I started questioning my feelings for Kent. Was the sense of comfort I had with him love in disguise? What about my life in New York with Robert? Was it a replacement for the relationship I'd abandoned when I left Providence?

Only my grandmother could help me make sense of it all. She believed in me more than I believed in myself most of the time. More than anyone else in my life, she saw beyond the restless child who couldn't find her way in the world.

I drove to her house and found her waiting by the front

door. The gray-shingled Cape Cod home had always been a symbol of comfort, even as I sat in the back seat of my parents' white and blue-striped Ford Escort at the age of eight. It was because of Grandma. It seemed she knew exactly when I needed her and how to make everything better.

As I approached her, I knew she could tell something was wrong. The fake smile couldn't distract her from the faint trail of tears on my cheeks or my red, puffy eyes. She reached out and held me in her arms.

"Let's go in and have a talk," she said, as she led me into the house.

I sat, emotionally exhausted, in that same living room I'd visited countless times. The fireplace remained off on that warm summer afternoon, but its presence was as warm and inviting as it had been when I was a child nestled under blankets on a chilly New England night.

Grandma handed me some hot tea, as had grown customary on my visits. "Tell me what happened? What's gotten you so upset, dear?"

Her eyes widened with concern.

"I met with Kent today. Years ago, I made a huge mistake. He was the one." I handed her the poem he had written about me.

She opened the folded paper and read the contents silently. "It's beautiful. When did he write this?"

"He meant to give it to me the day before I moved to New York. He's held on to it this whole time." I could feel my eyes welling up again.

"Isn't this good news, then?" She shook her head in confusion, and then realized the problem. "What's keeping the two of you apart?"

"It's too late, Grandma. He's married. It took me too long to realize how he felt. I never gave it a chance. Maybe I did love him. In my own way."

"I'm so sorry, my darling girl." She placed her shaky hand on mine. "You must be devastated. But, if you were truly in love with Kent, you would've realized it sooner. Sometimes, we can't help who we fall in love with and who we don't. It would've been so much easier if you were in love with him, but life isn't that simple—it's messy and complicated."

Part of me knew she was right. Even though I felt something with Kent's kiss, in comparison, it wasn't anywhere near what I felt when Robert's lips touched mine.

"Is there something I can do to help you feel better?"

I shrugged. "Will you tell me more stories about you and Grandpa. I remember how happy the two of you were." The thought brought a faint smile to my lips.

"I was one of the lucky ones, but even we had our differences and challenges over the years. No relationship is perfect, but what *is* important is mutual love, respect, and trust. Your grandfather had a big heart, and he shared it with his family. We came first before anything else in the world. Because of that, I never lost faith in him. He was the one person I could rely on, and that was the very thing that made me fall in love with him over and over again." She wiped a tear from her eyes that had started to form.

"Remember, my dear, the kind of relationships we build and foster determine the kind of life we live. A woman will always be happy if she surrounds herself with caring people who love her. The bonds we create are the only things that make our lives on this earth significant. Life happens. It's never exactly the way we plan it, no matter how hard we try. Our job is to make the best of the circumstances we're given."

"I thought the only way to make a good life for myself was to move away. Funny thing is, I never really had a good reason to leave. I've been wrong this whole time."

"We do what we think is right. Sometimes our hearts know what that is before our brains do. Don't be so hard on yourself, my sweet girl. We all make mistakes. Life is nothing but mistakes. It's how we pick up the pieces that really count. You'll figure things out. Give yourself time."

She went on to tell me about the struggles she'd had during

her marriage to my late grandfather. From one miscarriage to two job losses, and my grandfather's battle with depression when he was fifty, their life was far from a fairytale. What helped them get through it wasn't years of therapy or time apart, but rather love and trust for each other.

I had assumed their life was perfect, but like everything we encounter in life, there are cracks and bruises hiding below the surface. I felt privileged that she chose to confide in me like I had in her. In that moment, I didn't feel so alone. There was one person I could rely on, even when it seemed everything else was crumbling at my feet. I was truly blessed, indeed.

An idea popped into my head. "Grandma? Do you have a sketch pad I can use?"

After a few minutes, she returned to the room with a worn-out sketchpad in her hand, its cover a distressed shade of pale green. "I found this one in the attic on top of a pile of boxes. I put aside, marked with your name."

She handed it to me, and I immediately recognized it. The

pad was one of mine from high school. The last one I used before going off to college. I'd left it behind, hoping to leave my old life behind with it. I leafed through the pad, each page revealed sketches of tree-lined paths, old abandoned houses, birds soaring high in a cloudless sky, and the trail of Hunt's Mill that Kent and I often took. I turned the page and saw Kent's writing in the left-hand corner—*The beauty of nature is something we can never truly escape.*

It hit me. I knew what I had to do.

The next morning, I packed my things, eager to get on the road. Dragging two pieces of luggage with me—I never could pack light—I headed to Grandma's tiny oak kitchen ready to catch a good breakfast before my trip.

Grandma stepped into the kitchen as quiet as a mouse. As I turned to place my dishes in the sink, I caught sight of her. She had a surprised look on her face, and her gaze wandered toward my luggage, positioned upright next to the wall. "Are you leaving already?" A sense of disappointment crept into her voice.

"I think the best thing for me to do now is have a change of scenery. Actually, do you want to come with me, Grandma? It'll be fun."

"I would love to, but I thought you needed time for yourself. Won't I be in the way?"

"You're never in the way, and you know it." I smiled. "Plus, I think you might enjoy it."

"OK. It won't be a long trip, will it? I can't travel as much as I used to, you know. It's sad how our minds can have it all figured out at my age, but our bodies can't keep up." She shook her head and stared at her legs in disappointment.

"Not at all. It's just over the bridge. We're going to Newport."

CHAPTER ELEVEN

We took the fifty-minute scenic drive from East Providence to Newport. I marveled at the ocean view over the Pell Bridge that connected Newport to Jamestown and to mainland Rhode Island on I-95. The vast sparkling blue water was speckled with snow-colored sailboats and yachts. I had never seen a more breathtaking view. It was a painting brought to life. I had to use every ounce of will power to keep my eyes on the road.

"How beautiful!" I couldn't help uttering the words out loud. "I wonder why mom and dad never brought us to Newport when we were kids."

"I think your parents wanted to travel overseas and show

you girls the world. Rhode Island is the smallest state so people sometimes forget the incredible wonder we have in our own backyard. It's a shame, really," my grandmother replied. "Actually, come to think of it, your grandfather and I only came back to Newport once or twice after his parents died. I think it reminded him too much of what he'd lost. It'll be wonderful to see it again." She smiled contently.

"I'm glad you came with me, Grandma. Can you tell me more about my granduncle? I think it might help me figure things out. I hope it won't be too painful for you."

"Of course, it won't. I made lots of special memories with him here. What good are memories if we can't relive them? At my age, you never know how much time you have left, so every opportunity is precious."

"You'll live to one hundred, Grandma!" I said, more to reassure myself than her. I knew our time was limited, and in my mind, I tried to prepare myself for the day I would lose her forever.

We continued on RT-138 into parts of Portsmouth and

Middletown until we hit downtown Newport. We drove through Broadway Avenue. What once was considered the shadier side of town now welcomed us with trendy restaurant and sophisticated menus, appealing to both yuppies and hipsters. The street led to Washington Square where the historic courthouse and Newport History Museum were located. The historic charm wafted everywhere—from the cobblestone streets to the American colonial architecture of the Brick Market Building that housed the museum. Modern stores scattered nearby with gems like the Newport Opera House that was built in 1865 and now stood restored to its original façade.

We traveled around the corner to Upper Thames Street where the cobblestones continued, and the street stood lined with boutiques and specialty shops. We turned left onto America's Cup Avenue. The street that connected us to Memorial Boulevard. Our first stop would be the famous Easton's Beach or First Beach—as locals knew it—that tourist flocked to in the popular summer months from all over New England. As we descended the road, we were welcomed by the sight of a stunning crescent-shaped beach.

Its strong waves in a bright shade of blue were exactly as I imagined, only better.

We parked our car in the side lot and walked the beach, taking our shoes off along the way. The wind was strong and inviting, sweeping my hair to flow in the same rhythmic pattern of the ocean's waves. The warm and inviting sand under my feet felt surprisingly natural, although I'd never seen myself as much of a beach person before.

Grandma desperately tried to keep up as her feet sank into the sand, acting like weights and dragging her down. I suggested spreading out a beach towel instead of walking. She giggled in agreement. And although her body was weak and tired, her face had a glimpse of youthfulness, a transformation that mirrored the youth of her first time in Newport. We sat and watched the growing waves dampen the sand as each one came closer and closer to us.

The clear sky hovered over the water, reflected in the bright sapphire color on the ocean's waves. Countless tourists and locals reveled in the beauty of summer and sea.

A dark-haired man passed in front of us with two little boys. They laughed and smiled, having fun splashing in the waves, and I immediately thought of Kent. I held my breath for a moment but quickly shook the thought away. In its place was Robert. He would enjoy it here too, but only for a little while. Then his business obligation would kick in. I still owed him a phone call, but I had to figure out what to say first.

It would have to wait this time.

Right now, I couldn't think of another place I wanted to be.

We spent a few hours on the beach, enjoying the sound of the waves and the sand on our skin, before heading out to lunch.

"Grandma, do you mind if we go to La Forge's for lunch? I'd like to see where you first met James.

"I don't mind. It'll be nice to reminisce about those days. You shouldn't worry about me." She smiled reassuringly and placed her hand over mine.

We got to La Forge about ten minutes later. The outside wasn't what I'd expected. Grandma mentioned that the casino that housed the restaurant was the social club built in 1880 in the rustic Victorian-shingles style common in the area. She still remembered a lot about the area's history, even though she retired as a history teacher over thirty-five years previous.

Next to Crowley's Pub and the renowned International Tennis Hall of Fame, the traditional green awning on the storefront complemented the green trim surrounding the salt-weathered gray shingles of the building.

We entered the dining room and waited to be seated. I could tell the place had been there a long time. The dark-chestnut booths and trim along the mirrored wall gave away its age. My grandmother scanned the room and smiled to herself, probably recalling a happy moment she'd experienced at one of those tables with James or Grandpa. The hostess appeared and led us to the back and into a slightly more modern wing with a view of the tennis court.

Sepia-colored photos of the old casino in its heyday filled the walls. The pictures reconnected the locals to their rich history and that of their ancestors. It fascinated me how discovering where one's ancestors came from sometimes seemed to answer people's questions about their future. I smiled, recalling what I'd learned about my own family on this trip. Maybe this place would help me figure more out. At the very least, I had a chance to try the *stuffies* La Forge is known for.

We did more sightseeing, driving past St. Mary's Church, the church where John F. Kennedy and Jacqueline Bouvier married; Hanging Rock, the place where my grandfather and granduncle spent their teenage years; and Second Beach, where we ending our day watching the sun set over the water.

It must've been so strange for my grandmother to visit after being away for decades while she made a new life with my grandfather. I watched her quickly wipe a tear from her cheek, as she lay entranced by the movement of the waves in front of her. Her thoughts were lost among the tide, remaining forever unsaid to the world around her.

I placed my arm around her, my head gently resting on hers. My heart overflowed with a sense of peace as I shared that moment with her. I finally had the chance to comfort *her* the way she had comforted me so many other times. We sat on our beach towels in silence, staring out at the waves as they swayed back and forth over the sand. I didn't want to leave, but when the moon began to rise above the darkening sky, I knew it was time.

"I've never seen the moon look more magnificent than it does now, high above the crashing waves," I said in amazement.

"I have, my dear, in this very spot. And its beauty will never cease to amaze you no matter how many times you see it."

As early darkness set in, the moon didn't compete with the ocean, but became its perfect companion, reflecting its warm and bright glow in the rippling waves below. It created a peaceful and enchanting harmony that I couldn't easily forget.

I stared at the scene before me in awe. How incredible it would be to see this every night! As I gazed into the vastness of the ocean, I finally understood the significance of feeling small in the presence of nature. It was humbling and empowering.

A gentle poke at my sleeve took me out of the moment. It was time to end our perfect day, but my soul grew restless for more.

We got to our hotel in the evening, and after dinner inspiration flared. I searched for the sketchpad I'd made a point to pack. Once I found it, I stared at it. It had been so long since I'd drawn anything other than campaign graphics, that I was a little nervous I'd lost the talent for good. Flipping to a blank page, I began to draw, the sounds of pencil strokes echoed off the page and into the silence that filled the room.

I lay on the heavily padded king bed sketching for about an hour before a knock from the adjoining room sounded. My grandmother walked in after waking from a short nap.

I handed her the pad with a smile on my face. "Oh Rebecca, this is beautiful! It captures the very essence of the beaches—awe-inspiring and strong."

She handed it back to me, and I analyzed the picture I'd created to make sure it was exactly right. The side-to-side pencil strokes created the beginning impression of the water, one by one, combining to form the strong surf we saw at both Easton's Beach and Second Beach. The sharp lines formed the giant cliffs that peaked stately from the rippling waves. Curves and shading replicated the delicate sand's contours. The m-shaped curve of the distant seagulls captured the very essence of the ocean's vastness and wild beauty. I still had the talent, and now I had new inspiration. I knew exactly where to go the next day and grew eager with anticipation throughout the night.

CHAPTER TWELVE

The next morning, we headed to Empire Tea and Coffee on Bellevue—one of a few local coffee houses in the area—and tried their Aquidneck Latte, a coffee drink made with local honey. Like everything else in the area, it was surprisingly different, but soon I wondered how I'd ever lived without it.

While we sat there, Grandma talked about how things had changed since the last time she had visited. She emphasized that the important things, like the gorgeous views, the people, and the traditions, remained the same. Locals still enjoyed the beaches. Out-of-towners still flocked to Newport during the summer months. It was a continuous cycle that tied New Englanders together with their past. These were the things that would never change.

There was one more stop I wanted to make with my grandmother before our time in Newport ended. We got back into the car, turned right from the parking lot and drove to Bellevue Avenue, where we had lunch the day before.

The street was a gem of historic beauty. We passed many of the great mansions—or summer cottages, as they were often called by the former elites—that made Newport the place to be during the Gilded Age. From Kingscot, to the Elms, to Rosecliff, each mansion revealed a different architectural style from a time of great opulence.

Grandma reminded me that during the war many of the mansions were left in disrepair, but luckily, the Newport Preservation Society had saved them years later. It was difficult to imagine how anyone could abandon such masterpieces.

We continued driving past Rough Point, the house of renown socialite, Doris Duke, and followed the swerving road that led to the ten-mile stretch of road known as Ocean Drive.

The winding road took us on a roller-coaster ride among scenic views of coastal mansions with an occasional peek of the ocean on the other side. We drove all the way to Brenton Point, a lovely green space right across the street from it that was designated as a state park in 1976, and dozens of people flew kites, making the most of the ocean breeze. As we got closer to the park, the houses began to diminish, and in their place were crashing waves and seagulls. I couldn't contain my amazement and anticipation as we got closer.

We parked our car in the lot in front of the park and walked across the road to the benches facing the water. At each step, the agitated wind swept through our hair while the waves splashed against the cliffs, leaving a trace of ocean mist in the air.

"Wow! I never realized how amazing it would be up close. It's so wild and tranquil at the same time. I can understand why James was so drawn to it." I couldn't help being drawn to it myself.

"It's breathtaking," grandma sighed. "We're at the very edge of the earth. There’s nothing between the ocean and us as it melts into the horizon. How powerful and magnificent. Nature at its best."

"Isn't the water beautiful today, Grandma?"

I couldn't hide my awe at the bright blue tint of the water. As the wild waves crashed into each other, their rhythm subsided and they slowly lapped in a rippling effect, revealing specks of green seaweed hiding under its surface.

"Yes, it is. James asked me that very same question once. It's funny what you remember even after so long. Being here, I can see a little bit of him in you. You have that same excited look in your eyes."

"Really?" Pride pricked at me over my connection to a man I had never met but whom I found incredibly fascinating. I didn't know much about him, but from the stories I'd heard, he was a man with a good heart and a love for the wonders of the world around him. A dreamer, an artist, an individual without limits. Maybe I had some of him in me after all.

"Ready to head back, dear?"

I could tell from my grandmother's tired eyes and slumped shoulders that she needed some rest. I agreed to take her back, but I wasn't done enjoying Ocean Drive just yet.

This time, I headed back to the Drive by myself. I retraced the same historic streets and winding roads until I could hear the hum of the waves. As I opened the car door, the strong salty air rushed through me, and with it, an overwhelming calmness rippled throughout my body.

I headed to the same bench I'd sat on with my grandmother earlier, but the waves and dark emerging cliffs in the water called me closer. I'd gotten there in time to watch the sun set slowly over the crashing waves.

I crossed over the grass, and carefully stepped on the cliffs, one foot at a time, until I reached the tallest one that brought me closest to the water. It was as dark as midnight and incredibly slippery, but it was the perfect spot to take in the powerful waves of the ocean. I could smell the salt in the air, and exhilaration brimmed within me. The sky began to cast an array of warm gold and rose hues as the sun slipped past the horizon. The most glorious sunsets surrounding giant New York skyscrapers could never surpass its beauty.

At that moment, I could imagine James sitting on the same cliff, contemplating the consequences of war around him and the future he hoped to have with my grandmother. I don't think I could've felt closer to my granduncle and my relatives before him than I did at that moment. It was comforting and incredibly heartbreaking all at the same time. It was the first time in a long time that I didn't feel lost in my own life. That restless feeling that I'd tried to run from no longer settled as a pit in my stomach. Instead, it disappeared like fog after sunrise.

I took one last look as the sky slowly turned a darker shade of blue, and returned to the car. Holding the sketchbook I'd brought from the hotel tight in my hands, I looked it over. I flipped the pages and began to draw, inspired, like a seagull drawn to the water for sustenance. I looked past the dashboard and thought of

James with his camera, capturing stunning images of the glorious waves and rugged coastline like I was. He captured them through snaps of the shutter, while I captured them through strokes of a pencil.

CHAPTER THIRTEEN

The next morning, I told Grandma I would take her home, then head back to Newport. She seemed surprised at first, but as I expected, she didn't try to change my mind. It had been a common practice between the two of us for years. I would go to her with the determination of a mad scientist, an unbreakable focus that wouldn't be deterred until a hypothesis was proven. She would look at me for a second or two before simply replying, “Good luck my dear.” Each time, she identified my mood right away. Perhaps, something in the tone of my voice or the way I lifted my hair into a tightly set bun clued her in.

"You need the time to yourself. I think it's a great idea to extend your time in Newport. It'll help you clear your mind before you head back to New York," she said reassuringly.

"Actually, I'm not going back to New York." I stopped and took a deep breath in, not certain how she would react once I told her my permanent plans. "I'm staying in Newport. I think this is where I'm meant to be. I can't explain it, but it feels completely different from anywhere else," I sighed not sure how else to explain it. "I think I'm finally home."

Her eyes widen in confusion. "What about your life back in New York? Your career? And what about Kent and Robert?"

"Well, I'm eight years too late for Kent and not important enough for Robert. I might've made a mistake a long time ago that cost me my happiness, but I can't go back. The best thing for me to do is start fresh. I think a new place will help me move on. It'll take a while to get settled, but it'll be worth it."

"It's not like you to make such a rash decision, but if you're okay with it, then I guess it's fine. I can hear the excitement in your voice."

Without thinking, I pulled at my hair and set it in a bun.

"Good luck, my dear," she said with a smile. "Don't worry. Things always work out one way or another. You're not meant to be alone the rest of your life, if that's what you're worried about."

"Maybe." I wasn't too sure, but for once I wasn't too concerned, either.

"Did you love James?" I blurred out.

My grandmother turned toward me with a pale look on her face. I regretted bringing it up as soon as I saw her reaction. It was an abrupt question, but it was something I had been wondering about for a while and had struck at my thoughts ever since I'd learned the truth. But I didn't know how to ask it. If she had really been in love with James, how could she so easily move on with my grandfather?

"I did," she replied quietly, taken aback by my question. "I took me some time to get over him. I fell in love again in a completely different way." She smiled at me. "Love isn't always black and white, Rebecca. It's messy, inconvenient, and something you can't run from it, no matter how hard you try. Your grandfather helped me realize that. Although I loved James, he wasn't the right man for me.

"I believe James came into my life for a reason. If it weren't for him, I probably wouldn't have met your grandfather.

"Every relationship, whether romantic or not, teaches us something about ourselves. I have faith that you'll make the right decision for you. It's your life so you need to be happy with it; no one else does. You've always done the right thing before." She slowly got up from her chair and kissed my forehead.

I drove her back home and quickly packed my belongings. With one last look at my old bedroom, I knew it would still be there if I needed it, untouched by the passage of time like it always had been. I smiled. The big white teddy bear would be there next time I visited, with that same look of hope and contentment on his face.

I didn't have a place to stay in Newport when I got there,

but I'd make it work. It was out of character for me not to have a solid plan, but maybe a leap of faith was something I needed at this point in my life. In a way, staying in a hotel until I found a new place to live and new job was a plan—a very desperate one.

I'd managed to save some money over the years, despite having to pay a hefty rent for my tiny apartment. There had been plenty of days when I lived on stretched meals. It was something I'd learned from my grandmother's stories. She'd done the same when times were tough and money was tight, as had her mother before her. It was a lesson I 'd put into practice, luckily. I would need those skills until I was back on my feet. And those funds had to carry me through my rainy days.

The new possibilities filled me with excitement, but I couldn't deny the part of me that was terrified by the uncertainty. When I closed my eyes, it felt as if I were slowly heading toward a dark, stifling room without windows or doors to escape. I took a deep breath in and hoped I'd made the right choice.

As I ran to my car and drove back to the hotel, a text

message appeared on my phone.

It was Robert.

I hadn't heard from him since earlier in the trip, but it wasn't out of character for him to allow days and sometimes a week to pass without a call or text when he was out on company business. I tried my best to understand that business came first, but over time, it became difficult to stomach…that I was barely a close second. He would have to wait for me this time.

I spent the next few days taking in the ocean and the beach during the day and open-patio dining at the local restaurants at night. I saw men dressed in brightly colored Polo shirts, board shorts, and boat shoes, while women dressed in sundresses, sun hats, and high-heeled sandals that made them look two-inches taller. Locals and summer transients from the North sat relaxed in the salty breeze as they devoured New England dishes of clams, lobster, and other local seafood. They chatted and laughed as the sun slowly slipped past the ocean's waves, unnoticed. The golden ball of light melted into a rose-colored pool as it passed the horizon. I could hear the sound of the waves in the distance.

I sighed for a moment, thinking back to my life in the city. The lights and hustle were exciting for such a long time, but this had its own excitement, in a low-key, serene, complete kind of way. The nightlife didn't thrive on traffic and heavy crowds here. It was enough to hear the crashing waves, smell the salt in the air, and see the bright sunlight to remind a person that they were alive.

The following week, I found a small studio apartment with a balcony on Thames Street, close to local shops and restaurants. It was a great location in the middle of town, not too far from Kings Park, where I could sit on a bench, and enjoy an unobstructed view of the Pell Bridge overlooking the bright sapphire water. My apartment in New York overlooked crowded brownstones and gigantic industrial buildings on each side. But here, there were no tall skyscrapers in the distance or angry cab drivers swerving in and out of the city streets. In their place waited a quieter pace and gorgeous views of the water surrounding all of Aquidneck Island.

Instead of attending useless company meetings, I started

my day on Ocean Drive, a pencil and sketchpad in hand. The scent of the salty air woke me every morning, and the colorful sunset on Second Beach waved goodnight.

As soon as I settled into my new lifestyle, I contacted Robert. I couldn't ignore him forever. If I was going to put him behind me, I had to talk to him at least one more time. I took a deep breath before I called him one evening. Part of me looked forward to the sound of his voice, but the other part hoped he wouldn't answer.

He answered after two rings.

I froze, unable to vocalize any sound through my moving lips. I held my breath, as if one gasp would cause a chain of catastrophic events.

"Hi. I wasn't sure you'd call," he said.

"It's been a bit hectic here," I finally managed to say. “There were a few things I had to take care of. I had to find the right time."

Before I could continue, he jumped in.

"Well, I hope you've had a nice time. I wish I could be there, but I'll make it up to you."

It was something I'd heard too many times before, and the trickle of hope that first emerged when I heard his voice, transformed itself to disappointment. Nothing had changed.

He insisted on coming out to visit me since he was leaving for Providence to meet a potential client in the next few days. I agreed, knowing there was a chance I'd lose my nerve to call it off once I saw him in person. But I had to take the risk. Changing my life meant confronting him and the future of our relationship, no matter how painful it would be.

CHAPTER FOURTEEN

It was the weekend, only a few hours until I expected Robert at Empire Coffee. After breakfast, I drove to Ocean Drive and sat on the dark cliffs to collect my thoughts before we saw each other. It was a breathtakingly clear day with only a hint of dampness in the air.

I wondered how many times James had sat here before me, immersed in the ocean's presence. This place had been his refuge for peace and reflection, in the same way it had become mine.

From the corner of my eye, I noticed a young couple, twenty feet away, stepping from one tall rock to the other, all the while holding hands. At that moment, I envisioned my grandmother and James in their youth, doing the same dangerous and exhilarating thing. I couldn't help but smile and wonder what might've happened if James had survived the war. Maybe he would've taken me to this very spot as a child, and together, we would've reflected on the wonder and beauty around us.

It only took a few minutes for my mind to wander back to Robert and the discussion I planned to have with him in less than an hour. He wouldn't understand my rash decision for moving. He'd never done anything without meticulously planning it, and he did that so well. It was one of the things we had in common.

Everything he did was lavish and show-stopping, never missing a detail. He knew how to impress others, and people loved him for it. It was part of his charm, and it was what attracted me to him—that, and his magnetic smile that mesmerized me as much as a star-studded night’s sky.

He was a great businessman and could foster successful relationships with clients. Customers always chose Robert's company over any competitor, even when offered lower prices. It wasn't only his ability to offer a quality product, but the way he got to know his customers and anticipate their wants and expectations before they did that sealed the deal.

His friends could count on him for a good pep talk, but no one could get close to him, aside from his family. For someone whose demeanor was so inviting, a dark fortress surrounded his emotions. Very few people ever passed through it, including me. Every time I thought I was getting closer, I quickly got whiplashed back into place.

Would I tell him I was in love with the wrong man and had missed my only chance with someone who truly loved me? Maybe I was better off telling him I needed a change of scenery and no longer loved him. I never was a good liar. He'd see right through me.

I carefully stood up and headed back to the car. The drive to the coffee house was short, but my mind began to wander again.

When I arrived in the parking lot, I looked at my reflection in the rearview mirror. My hair was a bit wild from the ocean breeze and my cheeks had a slight rose glow to them. I patted my hair down to tame it, touched up my eyeliner, and applied my go-to paramour lipstick. It was a deep plum reddish shade that Robert often commented was his favorite. It reminded him of the red Nerium Oleander flowers that grew all over Sicily, and that he often saw in gardens on his trips there as a child. At first sight, they seem small and fragile with five delicate petals, but they could withstand the toughest of climates and still remain strong and glorious. The rock in the pit of my stomach grew larger as I stepped out of the car and trudged to face my destiny head on.

I sat closest to the wall at a table for two. For a moment, I thought about my time with Kent weeks back. It was a similar setting, but the two men were worlds apart. Kent was sarcastic, creative and philosophical, while Robert was refined, adventurous, and ambitious. I was lucky enough to have each of them in my life for a time—before they sifted through my hands like grains of sand. I shook my head to erase the thought and briefly looked up to find Robert standing in front of my table.

"It's good to see you," he said with a perfect smile, instantly bringing me back to the first time we met.

"Hi." I clumsily moved my purse and sketchpad from the table as he sat down. "Thanks for coming out here." I tucked my hair behind my ears.

"I've missed you." He took ahold of my hand and cradled it in his.

The familiar touch reminded me of life in New York. I couldn't help smiling and enjoying the moment longer than I should have.

"How was your visit with your grandmother?" He glanced over at my sketchpad. "Are you working on a new campaign?" He dropped my hand and flipped through the pages. "These are beautiful. Is that why you came to Newport?"

"The visit was nice." I hesitated a bit. "No, I didn't come to Newport for work." That rock in the pit of my stomach had climbed up to my throat now, and it held a tight grip. The words clung to the roof of my mouth unable to flow out the way they were meant to. Instead, something else popped out. "I want to show you something important. Will you come with me?"

He looked puzzled but agreed to follow me in his car as I drove to a place I thought might help him understand. Once there and out of our cars, we turned our gaze to the ocean that glistened across the street. He took hold of my hand, and we walked toward the cliffs.

"This is what you sketched?" he asked. "It's amazing! I understand the inspiration. My grandfather used to paint when he was young. He would go for walks in his town in Italy and paint for hours. His favorite thing to paint was the ocean. It's funny how perfect it is no matter where you are in the world."

"You never told me." I searched his face for an answer.

"You never asked." He gave a rueful smile. "I guess it didn't seem that important at the time."

I hadn't realized how little I knew about Robert's family beyond the successful immigrant story. How many other subjects had we neglected? I let the thought pass, and we sat quietly for a minute or two.

The seagulls called out to the horizon. Each caw lingered in the air like a deafening echo of what was to come.

"How about we take a walk and you tell me about your visit here?"

He caught me by surprise with his question. It had always been the other way around, as long as I could remember.

I told him how I'd come to that very spot with my grandmother and relived a small time of her life with James. This place was the link I had to a piece of my ancestry—the life of a relative I'd never met, but a person I had a connection to, nonetheless.

"And that's why I moved here." I blurted out loud, trying to avoid his glance. I closed my eyes, hoping the moment hadn't happened, that those words had only been said in my mind.

"You live here?"

He stopped in his tracks. I looked up to see anger and confusion on his face, something I had never seen and had hoped to avoid. "When were you going to tell me?"

"I'm sorry. I should've told you, but you were busy with your new opening. I didn't think it was important to you." It was a low blow, but it was time to reveal my anguish.

His puzzled look intensified as he gazed up at the sky. "Look, I know I've been busy, but that doesn't mean I don't love you. Where does this leave us, then? I can't move out here."

"I know." I was crushed.

For a moment, I thought he might've been happy for me. I'd hoped he was ready to go anywhere with me so that we could be together. But he didn't. Still, that was what you did when you loved someone, wasn't it?

But he couldn't.

And I couldn't live in his world.

Maybe *I* was the one who had been selfish the whole time. I was torn, but I couldn't deny the fact that Newport made me feel more content and alive than I had ever been.

"What can I say, Rebecca?" He moved closer and held my hand in his again.

The wind picked up and swept my hair in a dozen directions. He seemed less upset, but a hint of disappointment lingered in his voice.

"This place suits you. You're as restless as those waves out there. You try to hide it behind your plans and schedules, but I saw it every time we traveled together. Your eyes widened with excitement, and you smiled more. It's what I fell in love with the most. That and those beautiful dark eyes of yours."

He touched my cheek and moved in to kiss my lips. A familiar warm tingling rippled throughout my body as it had so many times before.

"Are you sure you want to do this? We have a life in New York. Are you ready to throw that away?"

"I don't want to, but I have to," I replied holding back my tears. "This is where I belong."

He looked down in defeat. "I still love you," he whispered, as he turned and started to walk away.

"But not enough," I said, loud enough for him to hear.

He stopped for a brief moment. My breathing stopped, thinking he would come back, but he didn't. He continued without a look back.

I was alone again, the wind and roar of the surf my only companions. I sat on the cliff for a while longer and stared at the water, listening to the cry of the sea gulls, my thoughts lost among the tide. Before I knew it, the sky filled with the vibrant hues of sunset. It comforted me for a brief moment as my new reality set in.

My new life had begun, but it was bittersweet. I couldn't picture my life without Robert, but I knew losing him was a possibility as soon as I'd made up my mind to move.

CHAPTER FIFTEEN

A month passed, and I started getting used to being single again. I'd met neighbors and started a new job at a local advertising firm. We only had a few clients, so the hours weren't nearly as hectic as they'd been in New York. It gave me plenty of time to spend sketching in my free time at the beaches and Ocean Drive. My nights became busy again as I met up with coworkers who soon became close friends.

We got together after work for dinner or cocktails, talking about the newest rumors in the office or the weekend events in the area. I was part of a great team who worked incredibly well together—a second family. I had never experienced such a thing, working for a global company in New York. It was good to laugh again, to reminisce with friends and my sister, Grandma, and my parents, who were no longer too far away to visit on a more consistent basis.

I also began researching the history of the area during World War II and found more information on James during his time in Newport. He had been an extraordinary photographer. There were numerous newspaper clippings with his published photos. He'd sent many of the photos he'd taken over the years to local papers before leaving for the war. His legacy was a part of my family's history, and now pride for it replaced that former emptiness inside of me. And it ultimately helped me understand a little more about myself.

I had inherited my granduncle's restless, idealistic and creative nature, but it took me some time to fully embrace it. That insatiable urge that I had repeatedly buried deep inside of myself no longer showed its ugly head. Instead, I tried to live in the moment as much as I could, and it made me happier. I finally realized the simple things that made me happy everyday were enough in life.

My past lay perfectly where it belonged, until one day when I received an unexpected email from Kent:

Hi Rebecca,

Hope you're doing well. It's been a while, but I've been thinking about you lately. You'll be glad to know that I've started writing again. I've found inspiration since the last time we met. Maybe it came from our rekindled friendship, or maybe my newfound dedication to my family. Perhaps both.

I can truthfully say that I'm happy now. I want you to know that I'll always love you, but I've also grown to love the life I have with my family too. Who knew it was that easy? (Yes, I'm being sarcastic.) This is where I should be.

I hope you find the happiness you're looking for—wherever it may be—with someone who can love you as much as I have.

Your lifelong friend,

Kent

I smiled, remembering the good times and hoped Kent found the happiness he deserved. It was a lot more than I could give him.

Sometimes, what's in the past needs to stay there.

It reminded me of something Grandma would say. Either way, I had the closure I needed and holding on to what might've been would have robbed me of the happiness I hoped to have in the future.

I thought about Robert, and where he might be at that very moment. I hadn't heard from him since he walked away at Ocean Drive. It had taken me a while to stop thinking of him every night without crying, but eventually I did. I hoped he was happy, wherever he was.

It was difficult to put him completely in the past like I had

Kent. Maybe because I'd never really loved Kent the way I loved Robert. I had been in love with the possibility of Kent, rather than the actual man.

Robert, on the other hand, was someone I couldn't get out of my mind no matter how hard I tried. At every party I attended, I saw him in strangers.

I'd see him in random places. The grocery store, or at the beach. I'd hear his voice or laughter in a man's voice across the room. Soon, reality would set in, leaving me heartbroken all over again.

I devoted any free time I had to sketching, trying to get him out of my mind. I took some drawing classes and managed to improve my skills at drawing faces, a skill I never could perfect in my teenage years. It was exciting, but somehow all the men in my sketches resembled Robert time and time again.

I decided to visit my grandmother one weekend, hoping she might distract me from my self-made torment. When I got to her door, she greeted me with her usual warm smile and hug—as familiar to me as my own reflection.

"I dragged out some old pictures I thought you might like to see," she said.

I was thrilled! I'd always had a soft spot for old photographs, but I couldn't think of anything better than those of my own family. Grandma handed me pictures of herself and her cousin Elizabeth during their time in Newport. The sepia-colored photos had that distinct vintage look, but the smiles on both young ladies were modern and fresh compared to the photographs of solemn-faced people found in museums and textbooks. The two girls posed happily together, arm in arm, like partners in crime up to some rebellious feat.

My grandmother's light-colored curls were perfectly set in place with a crystal hairpin, while a dark lipstick adorned her playful grin. She was dressed in a knee-length, floral dress clinched at the waist by a dark belt. She completed her outfit with cream-colored gloves and dark open-toe heels. Elizabeth, on the other hand, wore a gingham dress in a similar cut, her dark curls kept in place by a light-colored ribbon. She had a similar playful grin and smiling eyes.

We sifted through other pictures, some from my grandparent's wedding, and others from the time when my mom and uncle were children. Everyone looked perfectly happy together. We found some photos that were taken of my grandfather in the 1950s. One of them was a colored shot of him sitting on a recliner in a beige pullover sweater and tie, large black rim glasses, and a kid on each knee. He had a hearty smile, laughing as he looked down at the young versions of my mom and uncle.

"He was such a good father. I fell in love with him all over again every time I saw how patient and tender he was with them. He easily transformed himself into a little boy whenever he was with children, despite his usual serious and responsible exterior." A faint smile appeared on her lips as she recalled the memories. "I wish he were still here."

I ran over and gave her a hug. I thought of my favorite memories of him. I missed seeing him in his favorite chair, reading his newspaper page after page. No matter what topic he was engrossed in, he would drop everything once he saw my sister and I moving toward the living room. We'd run to him, and he would sweep us up in his strong, warm arms.

"Grandma, which picture is your favorite of him?"

"This one."

She handed me a black and white photo of Grandpa in a double-breasted black suit. His hair was slicked back and a handsome, gentle smile adorned his lips. He was surrounded by friends and family at a relative's wedding, he couldn't have been older than thirty.

His youth lay frozen in time in that photo. Everyone would share in that happy moment generations after, every time they picked up the picture. It was a true representation of who my grandfather was—a kind-hearted man who was there for the people he loved.

"Who’s this?"

I'd found an old picture of a handsome young man dressed in a military uniform. His light eyes were a striking contrast to his short dark hair. His chiseled chin and square jawline made him unforgettable. He wore a long-sleeved khaki-colored dress shirt, honorary ribbons and metals on his front pocket and a military cover on his head. I realized who it was as soon as the words left my lips.

"That's your granduncle James. He gave me this picture right before leaving for the war. He always told me he preferred being behind the camera instead of in front of it. But he also knew he made the perfect subject regardless, and he used that to his advantage." She smiled and sighed, recalling a special moment they'd shared.

His features were different from Grandpa's. James had a longer, narrower nose and larger bright blue eyes. The broad smiles were exactly the same, proof that the two men were brothers.

We spent the rest of the day reminiscing about our time

with Grandpa, and revisiting photos of the rest of our family. They went back several generations to the time my ancestors on Grandpa's side came from Portugal and those on Grandma's side came from Ireland. Looking at those people in the photos and thinking about the struggles and happy times they faced made them real.

The family resemblance was fascinating. I saw similar noses, eyes, and glances in relatives born decades after. Knowing we were all connected comforted me. Each person took their separate path in life, but were all connected by name and blood. How could anyone truly be alone when they were an extension of something bigger than themselves—a family that lived before them and one that would continue to grow with each new life?

I left Grandma's after dinner and headed back home. A cool hint of fall lingered in the air. I decided to take the route over the Pell and Verrazano bridges this time so I could catch another glimpse of the sunset over the sparkling waters before the days grew shorter.

I opened up the car windows, feeling the late-summer breeze through my hair. It would be a quiet evening at home tonight, but I didn't mind. I had plans to decorate my living room with the family pictures my grandmother had given me. Each one was unique by itself, but together they formed a link to my family's roots.

CHAPTER SIXTEEN

I grabbed my purse and coffee and headed to the car. I had no problem grabbing a quick breakfast sandwich on my way to work, but I never functioned without coffee first thing in the morning. When I got to the office, everyone seemed suspiciously cheery, but I didn't put too much thought into it until I got into my office. My coworkers had tied balloons to the doorknob and stuck a happy-birthday banner to the door.

It was a welcome surprise. With everything that had happened the last few months, I hadn't considered celebrating my birthday. When I was a child, my mom made a big deal out of birthdays. She often welcomed us home from school with birthday cake. The house would be fully decorated with balloons, birthday signs, and our favorite flowers. Mine had always been orchids. I was drawn to their contradicting natures—strength and fragility, simplicity and untamedness.

Sometimes, Mom would allow us to miss school on our birthdays. Those were some of my favorite memories. On those days, she would wake me up and reveal that she had taken the day off work and that we would spend the entire day together. She took me to the movies, the mall, or even to a museum or the zoo.

She did the same thing with my father. He never knew what she had planned, whether it was showing up to his office for a birthday lunch or baking him his favorite pecan pie for dessert. The only thing he knew was that she would surprise him every time. He told everyone that her spontaneity was what he loved the most.

I started my day at the office checking emails before diving into a big project for a client in Providence. My cell phone buzzed, and I scrambled to find it in my purse. It was a text, probably a birthday message from one of my old colleagues in New York. I clicked on the message icon.

It was Robert.

Happy birthday. I haven't forgotten.

He was the last person I thought I'd hear from. I didn't know what to make of it. Was it some cryptic message I had to decipher, as my imagination wanted me to believe or only a friendly gesture?

Robert never did anything without a reason.

I set the phone aside and tried to concentrate on work.

Around lunchtime, my coworkers insisted on taking me to lunch at one of my favorite restaurants on Broadway. By the end, we were stuffed and reluctant to go back to work.

Back at my desk, I dove into my work in hopes of leaving early enough to savor the sunshine and ocean before sundown. I left at four p.m. on the dot and headed to my car, excited to head out to Ocean Drive.

Overall, it had been a good birthday. I couldn't complain.

My parents, grandmother, and sister all called to wish me a happy birthday, and I had great work friends to celebrate with.

Only one person was missing, and in his place was a useless text message. Memories of the birthdays we'd spent together tapped at my consciousness.

Robert would always take me out to an expensive dinner, an evening of dancing, or a show at the theater, but at that moment, I would've gladly traded all of it for his company at home.

I arrived at my usual spot on Ocean Drive and headed out to the cliffs. It was a beautiful sunny day, not a cloud in the sky. The water looked its perfect sapphire color as the waves splashed back and forth on the dark cliffs. What a difference a year makes! Last birthday, I had been stuck in traffic, rushing home to meet with Robert. But this year, I was soaking in the sights, sounds, and scents of a little piece of paradise. It was bittersweet, like everything else these days.

The wind picked up and the waves splashed harder and farther up the coast. I jumped as it sprayed my face and blouse more than I'd expected. I stood up and turned to move to a higher cliff, and as I looked up, I saw a man glancing my way.

"I couldn't miss your birthday." He smiled sheepishly. His shoulders were slouched, and his hands were hidden deep in his pockets, as if willfully surrendering to something he could no longer control. It was a stark contrast to his usual confident demeanor.

I couldn't help feeling an overwhelming sense of joy and doubt. Could he be standing in front of me, or was it a figment of my imagination? The adrenaline in my legs kicked in. I wanted to run to him. To feel him in my arms again. I wanted his lips to ignite mine, and his arms to wrap around me for an eternity, but my brain forbid it. I stood there, frozen in my emotions.

"How did you know I would be here? Am I that predictable?"

"I know you more than you know yourself sometimes." He smiled. "This is the real you. I understand it now." He glanced toward the horizon, taking in the idyllic scene in front of him, with all of its sights, scents, and sounds. “I can't get in the way."

Robert moved toward me, carefully stepping from one rock to the other until we stood face to face. Something in his eyes seemed different. They were warm and inviting, but a sadness I hadn’t noticed before rested there. He looked fragile and vulnerable outside of the city without his obligations and responsibilities. It seemed he did know me, but I hadn't completely known him.

"What are you doing here? I thought you were gone for good."

My body kept me locked in place, as if weights strapped my feet to the rocks where I stood. Emotions gushed through my body—relief, hope, anticipation…fear.

"Do you want me to be?"

He looked deep into my eyes, searching for an answer. The confident man I knew would never doubt himself. It was a side of Robert I'd never expected, a vulnerability I'd longed for him to have so many times.

"I miss you," he continued. "I tried to forget you, but I can't. No matter how much I stay busy. Little things remind me of you. Owl knick-knacks, orchids, and the scent of your apricot shampoo are everywhere I go. I keep finding your favorite basil gelato, even though you always complained about how few places sold it. And black and white puppies—yes, black and white puppies are everywhere!"

He let out a defeated laugh.

I laughed with him, holding back tears as my eyes welled with tears. "And we both know you're a German Shepherd kind of man!"

"They are the most tenacious and focused breed," he said in a half serious tone.

"I can't believe you remembered all that." I couldn't hold the tears back any longer.

He hopped to the rock I was standing on and took ahold of my hands.

"I still want you. I want this to work." His stare was intent and honest, and his voice quivered as he spoke.

"Are you asking me to move back to New York?" I froze. Would my joy be short lived? My heart sank in despair. I didn't want to choose between a new life and the man I wanted to spend it with.

He hesitated for a bit before answering. "You like living here, and I want you to be happy. I always have. And I've been selfish, too caught up in my work. I never realized how unhappy you were until the last time I saw you, and I don't want to be the reason for that. I never deserved you, you know." He hesitated again. "I've had a difficult time completely trusting anyone since.."

"Cristina."

She would be the reason for our relationship's demise. I should've known. We'd only spoken about her a few times, but every time his ex-fiancé came up in conversation, Robert changed the subject. Her name conjured a negative vibe in the room. She was a bad seed whose ever-growing vine twisted its way around us, then sucked the air dry.

"She's the reason I haven't given myself completely to you. She broke my heart, but the biggest mistake I made was bringing her into my family when she clearly didn't belong. I blame myself for that. She cheated on me and played my family the whole time. I thought I was good at reading people, but I let myself get suckered in."

"I'm not Cristina."

I looked him straight in the eye. What else could I say to make him realize I would never purposely hurt him or his family? He'd reassured me countless times that his past was gone and forgotten, but apparently the scar was still raw.

"You're not. It's me. I'm the one with the problem. I hope you can forgive me."

"I already have."

I surrendered all hopes I had so desperately clung to. If things had to end, this was the best way. I'd found some form of happiness, even if I couldn't share it with anyone. I was luckier than most people.

Maybe that's what was meant to happen—James was meant to have a short life, and I was meant to live mine in solitude. We were related, and ultimately, our lives would parallel each other in one form or another. I had to rip the Band-Aid off sooner rather than later, if I were ever to enjoy my lonely decades ahead.

I couldn't bear to look at him. I turned my gaze to the water, losing my thoughts to the strong rhythm of the waves.

"Did you hear what I said?" He grabbed my hand, realizing I hadn't heard the rest of the speech he must have spent hours perfecting. "I'm ready to put my past behind me and focus on my future with you. I understand how much you love this place, and I think it's already starting to grow on me." He paused, then lowered his voice. "If you happen to need a roommate, I know someone." He smiled and took my other hand too. "I love you. I haven't said it or shown it as much as I should've, but I want to make it up to you, if you'll let me."

I touched his face to make sure I wasn't dreaming. His skin was warm and prickly from his day-old stubble. It was a look I was only privileged to see in between client meetings, when he wasn't his usual impeccably groomed self. But he was here, in front of me, as real as the cool breeze that swept through my hair.

He leaned over and kissed me as though we had never parted. Any doubts washed away with each passing wave. Our lips moved perfectly in sync, savoring each passionate touch. Our breaths melted one into the other, like the ocean enveloping the sand. *This is what love tastes like—every kiss and caress finally proves it.*

The peaceful sunset and the smooth flight of seagulls across the sky were the perfect backdrop for a happy ending. But life isn't a movie. This wasn't the end. And whatever headed our way, we would face together. Now our lives no longer hid behind misunderstandings and regrets. The road lay open wide for new memories and experiences. We were finally ready to take the journey together.

Robert moved into my apartment and we made a new future together. We reconnected better than ever before. I realized I hadn't known him as well as I thought. He wasn't the charming, ambitious man who had little time for anything or anyone else. He made an effort to open up more, and slowly Cristina stopped lurked beneath the surface. She left. Forgotten. Never mentioned when our tempers flared or our feelings were inadvertently hurt.

Robert decided to work from home on company strategy, and he hired someone else to manage the day-to-day duties. He continued traveling to meet with clients, but he invited me to come as his partner, which I did willfully when I was able to take time off work. He asked my opinion on many of his business dealings. To his surprise—but not mine—I was pretty good at it.

Our combined brainstorming managed to help the business increase productivity and reach out to new clients across the country.

As soon as we both let our guards down, we were able to

appreciate one another the way happy couples do.

Our daily routine wasn't anything fancy—dinner at home and relaxing on First and Second Beaches until the weather permitted. While I sketched the sand and crashing waves, Robert took a nap on the shore or rushed out for a swim. I couldn't remember ever seeing him so relaxed. It was a side of him he still left hidden from others but not from me.

I didn't think I could love him more than I already did, but every time he told me stories of his grandfather's love of painting and how his grandmother was dubbed "la soprana" while she sang and worked at the local seamstress, I felt even more connected to him. Everything finally came together, and for the first time in a long time I was completely happy.

CHAPTER SEVENTEEN

I brought Robert to visit my grandmother for the first time that fall. She greeted him warmly, playing her thirty-threes on the gramophone, just as she had so many times for me. He wasn't a big fan—preferring the rock-and-roll classics of Led Zeppelin and Pink Floyd to the swinging sounds of Glen Miller and Benny Goodman. But he was polite and respectful as he had always been with everyone he met for the first time.

"I can tell why my granddaughter is fond of you, and it's more than your handsome face and charming personality." Grandma smiled and pointed to his heart. "Your heart is good. You have the best intentions"—she narrowed her eyes at him, still smiling—"but you don't always express them the way you should. I'm glad you figured things out this time."

"Mrs. Simas, I'm sorry for the way I've treated Rebecca in the past. I hope you can forgive me. You mean a lot to her, and I want to make sure you know how much she means to me. I wasn't thinking back then. It took time apart from her to help me understand how much happier my life is with her in it."

He turned his head and squeezed my hand as I sat next to him. I couldn't help but smile and think how lucky I was to have two of my favorite people together in one room.

"We all make mistakes, Robert. If Rebecca forgives you, I do too."

We spent the rest of the visit looking at family pictures, and talking about family stories that had been passed down from generation to generation. Robert opened up to Grandma about his own family, and how important they were to him.

He only fought for his business because of his family's legacy. In that moment, I finally understood what bonded us together. It wasn't superficial attraction or similar interests, but the greater importance of family. For a long time, I thought his ambition was only for himself, but in reality, he was showing loyalty to his family the only way he knew how.

Robert met the rest of my family, including my parents and sister a few weeks later. It seemed the natural progression, and it felt strangely comfortable, like the silence of a winter's sunset. We visited Grandma's house regularly, and as the days got colder, we sat in front of her fireplace, enjoying her old stories. We walked the same path behind her house, as I had with Colleen as a child. This time, Robert and I walked in front, while Grandma trailed behind, slower and slower each time.

I saw the frustration in her eyes every time we stopped so she could catch up. During those walks, I envisioned my grandfather strolling beside her in spirit, an arm carefully wrapped around her waist. I knew her heart ached for him.

"Don't worry about me," she would say with a wave of her hand. "It'll happen another twenty times, so don't wait for me to catch up. My body's broken, and I have to make do with what I can and can’t do."

Then she'd stop for a moment, and cleared her throat, her voice seemingly softer and happier. "Don't let me spoil your time together. Enjoy your walk, and don't pay attention to the old lady in the shadow."

I saw the emotion in her eyes and the content smile on her face as I wrapped my arm around Robert's right arm, bringing him closer. He smiled and kissed my forehead, just as grandpa had done to her.

Life was as close to perfect as I could've ever imagined. My mornings didn't begin with a landscape of skyscrapers spread out among the vast gold-tinted horizon, like I thought they would. Instead, cool, salty breezes and the voices of passersby strolling to nearby shops greeted me as I dressed for work. A kiss goodbye from the man I had always hoped to have by my side sent me off on my day. The mundane routine of life was something I anticipated every morning, and its comfort lulled me to sleep each night.

My job grew even more rewarding because it allowed me the freedom to sketch, something I had been away from for far too long as an art director in New York. Robert's business grew and flourished, and all the while, my contributions were gladly requested. I became part of his family business, and it only proved he and I were growing closer and bridging the gap that had been present for so many years.

We got into the routine of a couple, with the perks of travel and the joys of enjoying life by the ocean. I couldn't have asked for anything more. I'd discovered the contentment and fulfillment I'd hoped to find in life. Maybe my granduncle, James, was looking down at me with a smile, vicariously living through me. I hoped so.

CHAPTER EIGHTEEN

We decided to go back to Monforte San Giorgio the following summer. It was early June, and the Sicilian weather was dry and warm. The lush green hills and floral-perfumed air were as I remembered, and I reveled in the beauty. We visited Robert's first and second cousins who lived there, in spite of its lack of opportunity and few modern conveniences. Their frequent smiles and hearty laughs reminded me that happiness was a state of mind and could easily be reached anywhere, even in a small town far from the hustle and bustle of the modern world.

There was something in the air that cast a euphoric spell on everyone in its path. It might've been the sweet scent of fragrant flowers that filled the morning air, marrying perfectly with the salt of the sea or the distant sound of the accordion played by a villager—its gentle legato melody unraveling the history of an ancient culture with its every beat.

In the afternoons, villagers leisurely walked the cobblestone paths, young and old alike. Children would skip down the path, giggling as they sang what sounded like nursery rhymes with every new step while their siblings quietly picked flowers by nearby bushes to place in their hair. Adults trailed behind, engrossed in animated discussions, their voices and hand gestures rising and falling in pitch and movement, as if mimicking a melodic aria performed on stage.

Elderly villagers took part in the ritual, as well. They walked in pairs, pointing and admiring the lush hills, perhaps reminiscing about the old days when life was simpler. Wide smiles adorned their delightfully wrinkled faces, reflecting those prized memories they had gained over the years. Each person greeted us in the same manner, with a smile and a nod of their heads, welcoming us to their little piece of heaven among the hills.

Robert's relatives were warm and giving people who treated me like a long-lost family member who had been away from home and greatly missed for years. Their familiar smiles were as comforting as the town's early sunrise.

They tried to communicate as best they could with broken English phrases that inevitably ended with the question "*si?*" Dark almond-shaped eyes eagerly reflected back at me while they held their breath for my answer.

"Si," I would reply, and my Mediterranean-featured companions would suddenly break out in shouts of exaltations, a sacred code deciphered.

It was a magical word that could clear up the meaning of those broken phrases. In truth, I grew to enjoy the sound of all those special words repeated over and over again—*bella, buono, mangia,* and *il mare*—each one a word that resonated joy to my ears over the fifteen days we were there.

We spent our days and nights eating fabulous meals al fresco, all with fresh ingredients from the garden and local meat and fish shops. It was Italian hospitality at its finest, and it would surpass the most elite Italian restaurant in New York every single time. Afternoons were devoted to strolls along the narrow cobblestone roads, often leading to hidden paths of stone ruins behind abandoned gangways. We visited Spiaggia di Venetico Marina—a serene beach with gorgeous views of the turquoise water. It was just past Parrocchia San Girogio Martire, a Stucco church with dark wooden paneled doors on Via Immaculata.

My favorite spot in town was barely past the church on Via Oratorio. The winding road opened up to gorgeous panoramic views of the valley. The majestic green hills lay wide and lush against the broad, open sky. Bright sunrays speared the large fluffy clouds as they stood out against the robin blue sky. It was a peaceful place that I couldn't help but visit when everyone was fast asleep during the daily siesta.

For one of our many day trips, we visited Isola Bella in Taromino, an hour and a half drive from the village. The small island was connected to the mainland by verdant evergreen trails, surrounded by a pebble beach and the clearest water I had ever seen. The sea had an abundance of colorful fish whose bright hues sparkled as the sun's rays bounced off their scales.

It seemed just another gorgeous summer day, but it was the day Robert proposed. There was no crowd of people, as I had always expected, but along the trail we walked, the birds and trees became our only witnesses. Simple and perfect.

CHAPTER NINETEEN

The next nine months were filled with wedding preparations. Our families spent time together around dining-room tables and at restaurant gatherings as details of the wedding ceremony and reception came together.

Before I knew it, the summer grass began to fade to brown and those bright green trees lined up in front of our apartment turned to warm shades of gold and red. The nights we spent along the ocean lessened as the air turned brisk and the winds grew stronger.

The change in seasons was something I had always loved. Throughout my childhood, I shrieked with excitement at the first budding plants of spring as well as the first vibrant autumn leaf. As a teenager, I would catch the first snowflakes with my tongue and feel the cold, wet snow dissolve in my mouth. The refreshing sip of melted liquid reminded me of the snow cones Colleen and I enjoyed every time our parents took us to the local summer carnival.

Back in New York, when I wasn't caught up in the hustle of everyday life, I would step back from the pedestrian-crowded sidewalks and hide under the awning of a local storefront. I watched the commuters rushing to work, intent on reaching their final destination as fast as possible. Their briefcases and computer backpacks were slung across their bodies and their shoulders were slouched. Not one of them aware of the fragile snowflakes nestling on their overcoats. But I would catch those first winter snowflakes and watch them slowly melt in the palm of my hand.

Grandma was excited about our wedding, and found every opportunity to talk about the details.

Her own wedding had been held in a simple chapel with

fewer than twenty people. She handed me a picture of her and Grandpa on their special day. They'd made a handsome couple. My grandpa was young and handsome in his dark suit and light gray tie, and my grandma glowed by his side. She wore a white satin gown with a high sweetheart neckline and long sleeves that ended in a point over her delicate hands. A striking lavaliere pearl and silver pendant hung around her neck. She'd inherited the Edwardian piece from her mother. It was an elaborate necklace that radiated elegance, especially when paired with her sleek and simple gown. The delicate chain shined as small iridescent pearls stretched along its entirety. Multi-colored glass jewels adorned the pendant in a circular pattern. I couldn't hide my excitement at the exquisite jewelry.

“How beautiful!” I exclaimed out loud.

Before I knew it, she'd left the room and returned with the necklace. She wrapped it around my neck, and I could feel the cool, gentle weight of the piece on my chest.

"It's yours," she said. "I wanted to give it to your mother for her wedding, but she preferred modern jewelry. In those days, young people despised anything old. It looks perfect on you, darling."

I was speechless. It was the most precious gift I had ever received. I gave her a quick kiss on the cheek to show my appreciation, and ran my fingers over the delicate jewels. Each stone shone under the lamp's warm glow, creating a spectrum of color across the room. It was the perfect family heirloom indeed, passed down for generations. And I was next in line to wear it.

It was an idyllic June afternoon, the sunlit sky a tranquil shade of light blue. The warm rays of sun were inviting, and the tepid wind seasoned the air with a hint of salt from the ocean's breeze.

The morning butterflies that had made their home in my stomach quickly turned to sparks of exhilaration as each hour passed. Robert had gone to the hotel to get ready, and I was left savoring my last few hours of life as a single woman. I didn't know what our future would hold, but despite our faults, we were drawn to each other in every way. From what Grandma had said throughout my life, these were the qualities that made for a happy, lifelong companionship. It was what she had had with Grandpa, and what I hoped to have with Robert.

I walked toward the front door of St. Mary's Catholic Church with Colleen by my side. The iconic church had a deep history of blessing the union of many couples since it first opened its doors to parishioners in1848. Among the more famous were John F. Kennedy and Jackie Bouvier back in 1953.

The gothic revival-styled architecture stood tall and distinct among Memorial Boulevard's colonial-style buildings. Its steep pitched roof, side tower, and arched windows were an architectural wonder, no doubt, but the interior led to an even more wondrous sight.

Stairs led to a narrow aisle lined with arches and columns on both sides—reaching out to a gigantic cathedral ceiling above. Every step beyond those front doors encompassed an overwhelming sense of reverence. The multi-colored stained-glass window panel above the altar at the opposite end shone bright as the sunlight peeked through each piece of delicate glass.

It was even more grand up close.

Colleen smiled in anticipation as she led me to the bridal room. She made a beautiful maid of honor. For the first time, I noticed how grown up she was. Her sandy curls were set high on her head, emphasizing her high cheekbones. I'd always pictured her as a little girl, running around with pigtails, borrowing my clothes…even as I watched her packing for college four years ago. Somehow, I'd missed her young adulthood until that very moment. Fifteen years of her life had passed right in front of me without my notice.

The fragrant scent of flowers and candlelight filled the church. Orchids were tied to the pews with snow-white ribbon, and small orchid bouquets were placed on both sides of the altar. Their bright magenta center faded from blush to porcelain as it reached the petals' ends. As I walked down the aisle with my father, I tried to breathe it all in—the smiling guests, my father's quick stroke of his cheek as he discreetly wiped at a tear, and Robert's dancing eyes as I moved closer to take his hand.

We faced the priest, our hands interlocked as one. The music stopped, and the powerful words spoken by the priest echoed from every corner of the church with a vibrating tone I felt throughout my entire body.

My mother and grandmother sat smiling and chatting with each other. It was one of those rare sights, like a blood harvest moon, unlikely to be seen for another twenty or thirty years. They loved each other, no doubt, but their interests were polar opposites just like their looks.

My mother's subdued features came from my grandfather. Her sad gray blue eyes and half-smile mimicked his. Mother's go-getting personality worked in favor of her love for the modern.

As an adult in the 1970s she loved progress and anything modern. "Nothing gets done if you always rely on the past," she would say when confronted by traditionalism. It made her a successful woman and a great role model, but she never found the same joy I did in listening to family stories about the past with Grandmother. Still, it was nice to see them together and happy—the two generations of women who made me who I am. Their bond had roots hidden deep beneath their strong personalities.

As Robert and I turned to face our family after our first kiss as husband and wife, applause and the jubilant sound of *Mendelssohn's Wedding March* greeted us. We walked outside and basked in the mild-June breeze ready to start our new life together. It was one of those surreal moments that I wanted to remember for a lifetime—one that my mom and grandmother each experienced on their wedding days.

CHAPTER TWENTY

The sky was unusually dark that September morning. I closed the front door behind me, noticing the storm floating across the carbon-colored sky, and hurried to my car. The clouds shadowed my every step. As I closed the car door, the rain unleashed its rage on my windshield, hammering the glass. I sat still in the seat, trying to look past the downpour, but the swooshing wipers only moved the rain from side to side, revealing a tiny glimpse of the street in front of me only once every three seconds. I waited for the rain to let up, then drove my car the short ten-minute trip, fighting the strange shivers racing down my spine.

My day at the office had started as it had every Monday

morning, with the grumbling of coworkers as they clenched their coffee mugs, complaining about their weekend ending too fast. The shuffling sounds of paperwork and printers filled the background, like the synchronized sounds of an assembly line running on a tight schedule. I reached into my purse for my office key, ready to finish a few pending projects on my to-do list.

By noon, my eyes were tired and blurry from hours of heavy concentration. I had tackled most of my projects, and now I was ready to enjoy a well-deserved break. I pulled the door behind me halfway.

The phone rang.

I tried to ignore it.

The shivers returned, racing down by back, telling me to answer the call. I picked up the receiver.

"Sweetie, is that you? It's Mom." I heard a shaky voice on the line. It was unlike her to call me at work.

"What's wrong? Are you ok?"

"Yes, I am. It's Grandma..."

She broke off, and her voice started to tremble. It was the first time since Grandpa's death that I had heard her sound so shattered. I froze.

"She's gone, baby, she's gone!"

Her cries grew louder and more painful in my ear. I held my breath. My heart beat faster and louder in my chest. I sank into my chair, motionless.

"Rebecca, I'm sorry I'm such a mess." Her cries grew fainter as she tried to compose herself. "Don't worry. I'll take care of everything. I know the two of you were close, so I called you right away."

My mother took charge in every moment of crisis. She had the strength and loyalty of a matriarchal elephant fighting for her young. I'd admired that quality most growing up. From helping Grandma take care of Grandpa when he got sick, to helping her best friend with a horrendous divorce, my mother was the rock that stood strong during troubling times.

"I'll be there right away."

"I'm at her house. Be careful driving," Her voice began to shake as she fought back tears.

I drove the forty-five minutes to Grandma's house on autopilot. Before I knew it, I was parked in her driveway. I froze and sat in the car for a few minutes, not sure what to do, unable to find the strength to move. Everything looked the same from the outside. Orange garden mums and deep-red pansies signaling the autumn season filled the front yard as always. Grandma never failed to keep her garden manicured and filled with radiant flowers.

I remembered helping her in the garden as a child. She would meticulously space out seeds and cover them up with soil and gentle taps of her fingertips. We would walk together, hand in hand, in the back garden, admiring all the flowers and enjoying their sweet fragrance.

"My sweet Rebecca, never forget that hard work pays off," she would say. "Remember how much time we took to plant our seeds last season?"

I would eagerly nod my head, my ponytail bouncing up and down.

"Well, look at the fruits of our labor. These enchanting flowers are our reward. We have to be patient, but our hard work pays off in the end." She would gently move a fresh-cut flower toward her nose, closing her eyes briefly as she inhaled the familiar scent. And as that scent filled her senses, a smile always appeared on her lips.

The memory slowly passed, and in its place, there was an overwhelming feeling of dread. My legs became leaden as I moved toward the door, as if metal stilts were strapped to my calves. I rang the bell, and my mom answered the door with swollen, red eyes. A faint trail of tears had left its mark on her cheeks. She quickly dried the new tears that had started to well in her eyes with the back of her hands. It was a sight I had only seen once before. Her sad eyes grew grim and vacant, as if part of her spirit had left with my grandmother's final breath.

I walked into the living room, and everything seemed the same. The familiar fireplace still stood there with its worn bricks, surrounded by those old chestnut panels. The floral armchair still retained that faded rose tint that I loved. It continued to stand tall next to the gramophone my grandma prized and played every night.

It all looked the same. I could imagine her sitting there now, with her eyelids shut and her lips mumbling one of her favorite tunes. How could it all still be there as if nothing had changed? It felt wrong for the rest of the world to go on without her.

I looked up from my ravaging thoughts to see my mother scanning the room as I had, locked in her own puzzling reality.

"They took her body. I'm sorry," she mumbled the words under her breath.

She stood there motionless, her arms enveloping herself as if holding her own body up to protect it from shattering into a thousand pieces upon the floor. In another moment, her arms melted down to her sides, glaciers breaking off into the surround water, overcome with warmth from the sun. She started to shake, her voice shrieking in bursts. Her eyes were bloodshot, and tears poured down her face as she looked at me.

My own eyes began to well, and instinctively, I reached out to hold her in my arms. I cradled her like the lost and broken child she had become, forever separated from her mother. Several minutes passed before she broke away and smoothed my hair with her hand and a broken smile. We went into Grandma's bedroom and stared at the empty bed.

"I thought she was sleeping when I came in. She seemed so peaceful. Her hair was down and flowing over her shoulders. When I got closer, I saw her pale complexion and dusky lips." My mother's hand trembled as she traced her own mouth.

We sat, silent in the chairs of the room's sitting area. It looked exactly as I had left it previously. For a moment, I hoped it was all a nightmare, but I couldn't escape the overwhelming sense of emptiness around me. It wasn't a nightmare. It was a horrible reality.

St. Sebastian Catholic Church in Providence filled with family and friends, ready to pay their respects to an incredible soul named Helen Margaret Simas. She was kind and talented, an extraordinary mother, grandmother, friend, and dedicated teacher. Her wisdom went beyond her years. Everyone present had anecdotes and tears to share about the woman they loved. Emptiness and anger racked my heart while I sat in between my mother and Robert. I grasped their hands, as if they too would slip away from me and wander between the world of the living and the dead.

I was lucky to have had my grandmother for so long, but I couldn't help but think of how cruel it was that we live on this earth for such a short time. The heavy incense in the air filled my nose. The overpowering scent mixed with the flow of my tears, making it difficult for me to catch my breath.

After the memorial service, we laid her to rest at Swan

Point Cemetery, a divine garden where headstones stood in harmony with the fragrant flowering trees, overlooking the Seekonk River, just as she had wished. It was the perfect spot for her to spend the rest of eternity, next to my Grandfather. Some might picture the place as heavenly. It was a true replica of Grandmother's spirit. My heart ached, knowing that I would never see her face again except in pictures and distant memories that each passing year eroded. One day, memories of her would be forgotten, like the many generations of ancestors before us.

Days and weeks grew more difficult as my grief set in. I was lost without Grandmother's presence. Simple things like red roses—my grandmother's favorite—would move me to tears. I would catch glimpses of older women and forget she was gone, until I discovered it wasn't my grandmother but someone else's.

The newly blossomed relationship between my mother and me helped me cope the most. We'd loved each other for years, but we never truly connected until Grandma's death. I began to appreciate her intense, independent streak, and she began to understand my strong emotional drives. She was a strong woman who hated to show any weakness and would only reveal her vulnerable side to a select few. Though I had inherited her drive, my emotions consistently got the better of me. As a result of Grandma's death, we spent more time together, and we bonded over stories of her. Mom found an appreciation of our family's past, while I learned more about hers. I was proud to know that one day, this woman would be my child's rock, just as Grandmother had been mine.

CHAPTER TWENTY-ONE

"Can you play it?"

"Of course." I reached out for one of Grandmother's old thirty-threes and played her favorite song *At Sundown* on the old gramophone I had inherited.

"I love it!" she shrieked with delight in the way only a child could. I grabbed her hand and we started to dance. I spun her around and she joyfully yelled even louder. I couldn't help but laugh. When the music stopped, she jumped into my arms and gave me a big wet kiss on the cheek.

"I love you," she whispered in my ear.

"I love you too," I whispered back, stroking her long sandy blond hair. I looked at her olive eyes and childish smile, and my hurt fluttered. She ignored my emotion and ran off giggling into the back of the house toward Robert in the kitchen.

She returned after a few minutes with her favorite lilac jacket. "Can we go now?"

"I don't see why not." I grabbed my purse and keys and headed to the car.

We drove that old familiar road with its winding turns. Her little head rose high above the car seat, trying to peek at the magnificent houses along the way. I reached the park where we often ran around playing tag and flying kites during warm, windy summer afternoons. She grabbed ahold of my hand and jumped out of the car. We crossed the street as the sound and scent grew stronger.

"This is a special place for our family. Your great-grandfather and great-grand uncle came here. Great-Grandmother did too. It was a special place for them and for me. When everything seems to change, remember that the ocean is life's one constant.

"Is this the place you and Daddy go without me?"

"It is. You were too young to come here before, but I think you're ready now."

The wind swept through our hair, the salty air refreshing and comforting. We carefully climbed the dark-espresso rocks, hand in hand until we found one close to the water but safe for a 5-year-old. We sat in silence for a few minutes as I held my daughter's hand. Seven years ago, I'd first stepped foot in Newport and realized it was home. So many things had changed, but this one place always remained the same.

I imagined James sitting on the same rocks seventy-five plus years ago, unaware of his future and spending some of his most memorable moments with my grandmother. I could see her with Grandpa as they built a love story that lasted over seventy years. How many individuals before us did these crashing waves inspire as their eyes stared far beyond the horizon?

"Isn't the water beautiful today, Helen?"

"It is Mommy." She grinned and gave me a playful smile and giggle. Her eyes danced as they reflected the sunlight bouncing off the ocean. For a moment, I saw a glimpse of my grandmother in her sweet face.

The waves continued to crash along the rigid shoreline as they had for my family—as they always would—as long as the ocean meets the horizon.

<<<<>>>>

ABOUT THE AUTHOR

Tammy B. Tsonis is a writer and poet. She was born in Bari, Italy, and migrated to Chicago, IL with her family when she was 6 months old. She grew up in Chicago and lived there until she was married in 2010. Tammy is also a mother to two boys and a military spouse. She has lived in several states and continues to value those experiences and relationships she's built along the way. She returned to Chicago in 2019, and currently resides there with her husband, sons, and two cats. When she’s not writing, Tammy enjoys photography and travel. *Lost Among the Tide* is her first book.

Made in the USA
Coppell, TX
29 April 2023